The Mare in the Trough

and other short stories and poems

Dennis L. Denman

PublishAmerica
Baltimore

© 2005 by Dennis L. Denman
All rights reserved. No part of this book may be reproduced, stored in a retrieval system or transmitted in any form or by any means without the prior written permission of the publishers, except by a reviewer who may quote brief passages in a review to be printed in a newspaper, magazine or journal.

First printing

ISBN: 1-4137-8068-7
PUBLISHED BY PUBLISHAMERICA, LLLP
www.publishamerica.com
Baltimore

Printed in the United States of America

Dedication

I would like to dedicate this book to my parents, M.L. Denman and Dorothy L. Denman.

I would also like to dedicate it to my wife, Sheri, and to our two children, Kristen and Melany.

Acknowledgments

I would like to thank Deanne Leonard, J.T. Ellison, Sandy Lowe, Cherie Hopkins, and Roy Parker for their encouragement and reading some of my works; and taking the time to give sincere comments regarding these writings.

I would also like to acknowledge the love of God in my life, without which none of this would be possible. I would hope when I am gone from life on this earth it may be said I was true to the calling: True to the calling of veterinary medicine, and true to the calling of God through Jesus Christ.

Table of Contents

Evelyn Louise	8
Compliment to My Dad	9
The Child	10
Many Parts, One Function	11
James Walker	12
Second Fiddle	13
Beyond The Surface	14
Unable to Speak	15
The Scar	16
Interruptions	18
"Religious People"	19
A Young Person's Prayer of Reality	20
"Perfect is the worst enemy of Good"	22
Observation	23
Sensitivity	24
Speaking to Others	25
Children	26
Asking For Help	28
Stormy Waters	29
Alex	30
Enjoy Them Now	31
Appreciation	32
Clear, Silent Night	34
Strength of a Workhorse	36
Surprise Packages	38
Survival	40
Things, Friendship, and Faith	41
Allowing Children to Grow	42
Listening	44
Beautiful Living	46
The Mare In The Trough	48
Full Circle	50
May 14, 1994	51
Shadows	52
Responsibility	53

How Do We Treat Others?	54
What's in a Can of Beans?	55
Cooperation	56
Standing Before The Cross	58
Special Days and Friends	60
Christmas	61
New Beginnings	64
Judging Others	65
Solitude	68
April 23, 1995	69
Men's Retreat	71
Scratching For Seed	72
Frustration	74
Tears of the Old Horse	76
Would We Be Recognized?	79
How To Live	80
Be Thankful	81
Tradition and Ambition	82
Cat Fights	83
Choices	85
Randy	86
Families (Mom and Dad)	88
Family Reunion	90
What Are You Going to Be?	94
Christianity	96
Focus	97
July 4, 2000	98
Making It through the Storm	100
Devil's Claw	102
Christian Service	104
The Best Way to Live	105
August 17, 2003	106
Follow Your Heart	108
Planting Seed/Going Home	110

Evelyn Louise
(February 23, 1979)

Dear God, you bless our home today
with a newborn child that comes our way.
We recognize she is not our own,
but one of yours in our care,
for a while to stay.

Please grant her mother and father
the patience they need,
that through each and every loving deed,
as she grows, they may guide her
in the way You would have her go.

May they surround her with a loving glow,
to provide her strength as she grows.
May it be given as love from You,
strong, sincere, and true.
Knowing that as it is given,
it comes through their hearts from You.

As she grows, may she understand
the loving hearts and the guiding hands
that without concern of their own
freely provided a loving home.

Compliment to My Dad

When I was a very young child, there was only one television broadcasting station in Corpus Christi. As I remember, programming was very limited, and they didn't have enough programs to fill the daytime hours. TV stations would fill some of those hours with live broadcasts of local events.

The local station would allow you to have your birthday party broadcast. A friend of mine had his party on TV, and I was invited. During the party, a person with the station would go down the line and ask each small child, "What do you want to be when you grow up?" At the time, a typical response for boys was, "a fireman," "policeman," or "a railroad engineer." When they came to me, I replied, "a daddy."

I have been told of the incident by my parents and by neighbors who saw and heard me that day. Looking back, I realize it is probably the best compliment I ever gave to my father. I can think of no other that even comes close.

How can we live with our children, so when asked what they want to be, they might reply, "a mommy" or "a daddy?"

When making telephone calls after our first child was born, I called my parents and told them, "I finally made it. I'm a daddy."

The Child

Did you see the child
inside the man,
When so beaten down by life,
he could not stand?

Did you see the pain
when he lifted his eyes,
And see the child
begin to cry?

Did you see his hand
begin to shake,
When he lifted it up
for you to take?

Deep inside each
one of us,
Is a child who needs
a hand to clutch.

Dear God, give me the strength
to extend a hand,
To allow a trembling child
to get up, and with me
as a brother stand.

Many Parts, One Function

People who have lived in South Texas for a number of years and driven beyond the city limits during the summertime have seen a combine in the fields. During the short grain harvest, they are a common sight.

The combine is a large, complex machine with many moving parts. When all of the parts are working well, the harvest is smooth. If some parts are not working well, the harvest is less efficient or comes to a sudden halt.

Most farmers make a thorough mechanical check of their combines, before going to the field, to prepare the machine for harvest. During the pre-harvest maintenance check, and when breakdowns occur, worn or broken parts are repaired or replaced.

Over the past several years, the elders have guided our church family along certain paths in preparation for the harvest. In the church family, we don't discard worn parts. It is the responsibility of everyone to be alert to those individuals who are overloaded. We each need to be ready to offer help or even take the place of someone, to ease their load, allowing them to rest from a particular job.

We sometimes become weary with a good work and need someone else to carry the load for a period of time. With a periodic rest, the Spirit is refreshed.

Have I offered to help someone, to ease their load, in a specific area of service?

James Walker

When we come in every Sunday morning, we always take a quick glance at the front row to see if he is in his place.

Just to make sure we see his tanned face and that head with hair of grey.

We know not his past—and it really doesn't matter—because we are blessed by his presence there.

Just to hear that "amen" which affirms an eternal truth spoken and to see his head nod when good words are spoken.

To see his head bow getting ready to pray, we know not what he will say, but we know he truly talks with God.

As he prays, we hear his voice shake, and deep within our souls, we feel our hearts quake. The lump comes in our throats, and tears well up in our eyes, because we know it was with God he just spoke, and when that prayer is done, we breathe a heavy sigh.

Yes, we will always take that quick glance to make sure he is in his place, for we know we will be blessed by his presence there, because it makes a little joy come to our hearts to know he is doing his part.

Second Fiddle

In this world, there are those people who are always out front at the head of the pack. We can all think of a few. These people have that extra measure of energy, self-confidence, and drive that makes them strive for a higher level of achievement than the rest of the crowd. That great mass of humanity that makes up the rest of the crowd gets to play "Second Fiddle."

The few people out-front get certain rewards that do not belong to the rest of the crowd. They are in positions of leadership and receive honor, glory, and praise for their work. We need these people, and they play a vital role in the daily lives of others. Sometimes, we tend to focus on their achievement to the point where we forget about the great majority of humanity . . . the rest of the crowd that plays "Second Fiddle."

If we think about it, we can remember that individual who had the most beautiful soprano voice and could sing a solo of great beauty. It is also true that you can take an average soprano from a school or church choir and put her with an average alto and have a sound that is truly beautiful.

We have heard the highly skilled trumpet player who could make melodies come from the horn in rich flowing sounds. We have also seen two amateurs play the same tunes with a second part and produce a beautiful sound that would have been impossible for either one to make if playing solo.

We have seen a man and a woman join their lives in marriage and achieve far more than either one could have done separately.

To all the people who have, and who continue to play "Second Fiddle," you do not have the leadership, honor, and glory in this life. The world is a much better place because you give beauty, harmony, and tranquility that add to the fullness of life and enrich the spirit. This is the role provided by God to the great majority of mankind.

Beyond The Surface

We know that we live in him and he in us, because he has given us his spirit.
(John 4:13)

Most everyone has sat behind a small child in church and watched him squirm. If his mother is not watching too close, he is soon turned around and looking at you. Finally, you make eye contact and smile, and the child smiles below the back of the seat. The God-given spirit dwelling in the child is plainly seen in his eyes and facial expressions.

The God-given spirit dwelling within older children, youth, and adults of all ages is often not seen as easily because of distractions such as funny hair style, different jewelry or a feeble voice or weak handshake. In our assembly at church, we are often able to look beyond the distractions to see the spirit within.

Our daily routines put us in contact with many people from all walks of life. In these people, there is also a God-given spirit, and there are also some of the same distractions we see in people on Sunday morning, as well as some others. We often do not see beyond the distractions to see the spirit within. Do we try as hard to see beyond the distractions Monday through Saturday as we do on Sunday?

Did I fail to see the spirit within someone this week because of shabby dress, poor manners or bad language?

Unable to Speak

The dog was paralyzed in both rear legs, unable to move or feel its limbs. The displacement of the fractured spine was obvious. I had seen this kind of injury numerous times before, but this time was different.

Across the exam table from me, stood the mother, father, and a young boy with red hair and freckles on his face. The dog belonged to him. I gave a truthful evaluation of the injury and at the same time offered to treat the dog with pain killers and anti-inflammatory drugs overnight to allow the family some time to make the decision they knew they must.

It was obvious the parents wanted the decision to be made at that moment but were unable to do it themselves. To may surprise, they turned to the boy and said, "It's your dog. You decide what to do." The burden was suddenly his alone, and he began to cry, and tears came to my eyes. They told him to quit crying and decide.

The boy held back his tears and decided to have to the dog put to sleep, and one of the parents signed a release to allow me to put the dog out of its pain and suffering. The boy turned to walk toward the front door and then stopped with his back toward me. He began to cry again, and his parents told him to stop.

I wanted to tell the boy to come to me so I could hug him and cry with him, but my eyes were full of tears and words would not come out of my mouth. Just as I decided to step around in front of the boy to hug him, he ran out of the front door, and his parents followed. I closed the door, and tears ran down my face.

When a lack of emotional strength does not allow us to speak, do we sometimes fail to act quickly enough and miss the chance to help someone?

The Scar

At first I saw him from afar
from there I could not see the scar.
Then I saw him closer in
and saw the scar across his chin.
Next I saw him face to face
and saw where each scar had made its trace.

We visited often and soon became friends,
and I realized the worst scar was deep within.
It was the result of terrible sin,
and I wondered who inflicted it, and when.

We became closer still and I finally saw
the trouble deep within was not a scar,
but a deep unhealed wound.
Yes, it was the result of terrible sin
not from outside but caused by him.

The sin that caused the wound
was his lack of forgiveness
of the faults and actions of others.

Was he some "worldly" person about whom
we are often warned?
No, he had often gathered under the roof
with "God's People" and had a smile so warm.

I don't know when it finally happened,
whether we would call it a moment
of strength or weakness,
But he finally understood why he had
the wound deep in his heart.

He began to truly look at the heart and
life of Jesus, and realized he must forgive
as Jesus had so long ago.
He sought the heart of the Savior and
learned to forgive others, and now
he can truly call them sisters and brothers.

The wound in his heart finally healed,
but unlike his face, it has a smooth finish.
Jesus, as in times long ago,
heals completely and without blemish.

Interruptions

The morning at work had gone smoothly, and I had scheduled an afternoon call south of Robstown.

I left the clinic that afternoon and was right on schedule. I was driving south on U.S. Highway 77, and as I approached my turn-off, I noticed a car with a flat. It was approximately fifty yards past where I needed to turn. Before I got to the turn, I saw a well dressed, middle-aged lady get out of the car. She looked at the flat tire and then looked my direction.

When things are going smoothly at work, do we sometimes view opportunity to do good as an inconvenient interruption?

"Religious People"

Do not from fear refuse to come near,
Though as a stranger I appear.

Don't pass by on the other side and
In your building run and hide.

Don't refuse to let me in,
Because in my life you see the sin.

I am the man up in the tree,
Your Savior came and ate with me.

I am the woman at the well,
My entire past He could tell.

I was the one they were ready to stone.
He showed them their sin, and sent me home.

We were uneasy with the "religious" people of our day.
They condemned us and did not show us the way.

Your savior could see our shame and disgrace.
He came to us and showed mercy and grace.

Today, there are still "religious" people, and we are still uneasy around them. The Christ is no longer physically among us. It is only through individuals in His living body that we can be shown mercy, and in turn, be led to His healing grace.

A Young Person's Prayer of Reality

Dear God, I don't know how to pray,
this, or that, or some other way.
In your word You show us how,
it's just so hard to do right now.

Worship . . . "What is worship?," I ask myself.
Something done so well, but always by someone else.
If only faith and God I could touch and see;
like shoes and clothes and cars and all the
other things that mean so much to me.

Fairness is the thing this world most needs,
but given the chance, I often take advantage
of others just to "succeed."
About this world and fairness you said:
"in this world you will have trouble"
"it rains on the just and on the unjust"
"the poor will always be with you"
I only have to look around to see that my
ideal world of fairness only exists in my dreams.

You sent your son to earth as man,
so all my plight you understand.
I know if through your strength I endure,
in my heart I'll be made pure.

If I look to You I know,
as the years so swiftly flow,
In your love I will be made whole
and on to my reward will go.

I wrote this prayer with some young people in mind, and that is the reason for the title. The more I think about it, the more I think it applies to people of all ages.
Does the turmoil of daily living sometimes overshadow the truth we know in our hearts?

"Perfect is the worst enemy of Good"

The above words are not mine, but those of a man older and wiser than myself. I first heard him say them two or three months ago, and I didn't think much of it. Since then he has said it two or three times, and I have thought about it and believe he is probably correct in his observation.

How many times have we failed to invite someone home for dinner or to visit because the house was not in perfect order? Have we sometimes not attended a class because the topics discussed did not perfectly fit our life situation at the time? In teaching our children, have we taken good things they have done and reworked them until near-perfect in order to impress teachers or other adults?

In today's language, we hear "Super," "Great," "Fantastic," "Fabulous," and "Class Act" so much that "Good" has lost its meaning. Our children have heard these words so much that when you say "Good," they sometimes think they have failed or are inadequate. Our children are also told that in whatever they do, "Be the best." In each endeavor, there is only one "Best," and many who are good.

Are we teaching our children good values concerning "Perfect" and "Good?" What did God observe after finishing parts of creation?

Observation

During our stay at Mo Ranch this summer, our family took a hike on the nature trail. We took our breakfast along and stopped by the pools of water, coming from a spring, to eat. I guess we stayed in that one spot for an hour, and the longer we stayed, the more we saw.

Initially we had seen some tadpoles and skate bugs running across the water. The longer we watched, the more forms of life we saw in the pools of water. One type of bug appeared to be debris on the bottom of the pool, and we finally realized it was present after we had been there for nearly an hour. Had we not sat and observed, we would have seen only one-fourth the number of creatures that we saw that morning.

In our every day lives, we might be surprised to see how much we have missed if we would but stop and observe our surroundings for a while. What might we discover if we stopped and observed our personal families for an hour?

Sensitivity

Do You Remember:

The first time your first-born child cried after you brought him or her home from the hospital?

The first time you heard an emergency vehicle with a siren other than the old kind, or a fire truck with a big, loud horn?

The first time you saw an ambulance or an airplane with strobe lights?

The first time you heard the warning horn on the back of a piece of heavy equipment to let you know it was backing up?

The first time you heard an auto alarm or a burglar alarm on a house in your neighborhood?

Chances are, you stopped suddenly, looked quickly, and felt an adrenalin surge when you experienced the things listed above for the first time. Now, they might get your attention, or barely turn your head. Our world has gotten louder over the years, and it seems it takes more shocking noises to get our attention. Our senses have been blasted to the point that they can no longer detect the things they were designed to perceive.

Do you remember when you were introduced to someone the first time you met with your church group? Do you remember the last time you introduced yourself to someone new? Is it just as vivid in your memory? Do you remember meeting someone on the sidewalk, making eye contact, and exchanging a smile and a greeting? Do you remember passing someone on the sidewalk, looking to make eye contact during their approach and passing, and they never looked your direction even though you passed within two feet of one another? Do you remember the difference in how you felt?

At church, at work and at home, how can we keep our sensitivity toward others near what it was during our first-time experiences?

Speaking to Others

One word may be to someone
A flag of hope unfurled.
One kiss that two remember
Can reach across a world.

One tiny seed awaking
Brings springtime to the clod.
One star can brighten midnight
One prayer can summon God.

(author unknown to me)

Three or four years ago, I was in a laundromat and saw someone who had been in high school the same time I was. He didn't recognize me, and we had not seen one another for twenty years. I finally went up to him and introduced myself. After exchanging greetings, he began to talk.

After graduating from high school, he had been in Houston working as a machinist. It was a good job, and he was making a good living. He told me he had suffered a mental breakdown, undergone some treatment, and was now living back in this area on disability income. I could tell from his physical appearance and manner of speaking, life had been difficult for him.

We talked for ten or fifteen minutes, and I could see a change in him as we talked. Just the fact that someone recognized and spoke to him improved his outlook, and I could tell the difference in his voice and on his face. I was glad I spoke to him.

When people do not recognize us, do we miss chances to do good by not speaking to them?

Children

Train a child in the way he should go,
And when he is old he will not turn from it.
(Proverbs 22:6, NIV)

We need to do fewer things *for* our children and do more things *with* our children.

As parents in the United States, we tend to be very good providers, and often times, very poor teachers. We have all seen examples of people wondering why a particular child turns out bad, and at the same time comment that the parents gave the child everything he always wanted or could ever need. In the same breath, the person will say the young person is lazy and won't work.

Most chores around the house can be done faster and better by an adult. If we have a child helping, it is often slower, and the end result may not be quite as good. Teaching and learning take longer than doing a task you have already mastered. We cannot tell a child how to do something and then expect him to do it well without first going through the process with him. We are to teach our children well so when they leave home and we are no longer around, they can provide for themselves.

Jesus could have done most everything for his disciples and told them what they needed to know, but I don't think you see much of that recorded in the Bible. He was with his disciples, ate with them and worked along side them. He allowed them to participate in things he could have done much better by himself. He was a teacher to them, and I believe there is even record of times when he was frustrated with them for their slow learning and lack of self-discipline. He was preparing them for a time when he would not be around.

Jesus spent periods of time teaching his followers in places where there were few or no distractions. Even in those circumstances it took a fair amount of time for him to teach them certain things. We often try to teach our children in the presence of major distractions; then we wonder why they aren't learning.

As individuals, and as a group, we need to look to Jesus to learn how to teach and raise our children. We need to pray to God for the wisdom to teach them properly and then take action to discipline ourselves to be good teaching parents.

In what ways can we better teach our children in the coming days?

Asking For Help

A number of years ago, I was injured by a horse. I was taking every precaution the circumstances demanded, but the horse did something unusual, and I ended up getting crushed between the horse and a pipe rail fence. It knocked the breath out of me and injured my leg. My vision was blurred for approximately twenty minutes. My chest, abdomen, head, and jaws hurt. I felt bad enough that I called in on the two-way radio before leaving the place and told my secretary where I was, the route I was going to take home and how long it would take me to get back. I also told her to send her husband to get me if I was not back in the specified length of time.

In our daily lives, we are sometimes physically injured or sick. We can also be spiritually injured or become spiritually sick. During physical illness, we will go to the doctor and then take the necessary steps to get healed. There are also times when we are spiritually ill, and the cause is obvious. When we recognize the cause, we can take the necessary steps to restore our spiritual health.

There are times when we become physically or spiritually sick due to unusual circumstances that may be beyond our control. During times like these, we often need to inform others of our situation and then depend on them and depend on God to see us through on the rough road that lies ahead. We still need to do our part to try to get back to health, but we need others and God standing by to pick us up if we cannot make the journey back home by ourselves.

Stormy Waters

During the eighth grade a friend of mine and I built a boat. It had a flat bottom and did not sit very far down in the water.

We went to the lake one day with his dad. His dad stayed onshore, and we set out in our boat early in the morning when the water was calm. We paddled it to an island in the lake to fish and explore the island. We spent most of the time on the downwind side of the island enjoying our outing. In the middle of the afternoon, we decided to head back to the shore. We didn't realize the wind had started to blow hard while we were on the other side of the island. We paddled as hard as we could but never made it more than forty feet from the island.

We finally removed a wooden gate from a corral on the island, strapped our life jackets to it, and then swam the two or three hundred yards back to the main shore while holding onto the gate. My friend's dad was not happy with us (he was mad) for not keeping a closer watch on the weather conditions.

We caught some bait fish with a net and gave them to their lake-front neighbor. For that, he agreed to take us to the island and tow our boat back. It was the only time our boat crossed the water with any speed.

Do we sometimes sail in calm water only to come around a bend in life's road and find we are in the middle of stormy waters? How can we be more aware of our surroundings and avoid such situations?

Alex

When I was in the second grade, we got a new student in our class. He was from another country and had been adopted by a family in our community. I was told to sit next to him during reading to help him with words if needed. We became friends and played at one another's homes on occasion. He even went to Papalote with us a few times (where my parents now live). We went to school together from second grade through high school. During high school, I was aware that things were not always good for him at home, but we didn't discuss it at the time. He and I weren't always real close, but we were always friends.

We didn't see one another until ten years after high school graduation. A couple of years later, we had more frequent contact, and he asked about my parents several times. I asked him to come to my parents' house one day. We went and spent the afternoon looking around their place at the big old oak tree and the gully in which we used to play. We ate supper with my parents, and visited for a while, and then came home. On the way home, he said, "Dennis, it was so good to visit with your parents and see their place again. It brought back a lot of good memories."

My friend isn't here any longer. While he was here, he did touch a lot of lives by encouraging people and smiling every time he led singing for our congregation.

Do we understand the importance of friends even when there may not be close personal contact for years at a time?

Enjoy Them Now

Not too long ago, our children and I were doing some painting. They were standing on boards across the top of two saw horses, and I was around the corner of the house painting from a ladder. I had given them each a paint bucket and a brush and got them started. I then went around the corner and started to paint also. It didn't take five minutes for it to start, and it continued over the next few hours until we finished the job.

"Daddy, she's not painting like you told us to."
"I turned my bucket over."
"She's getting paint in her hair."
"My neck hurts from bending it so I can see."
"We need more paint."
"We need to move over to another spot."
"Daddy, come here."

During the first few minutes, I became frustrated making trips up and down the ladder and around the corner of the house to see what was needed. After that, I didn't mind it so much. I realized that some day in the future, I would be glad to have a ten- and twelve-year-old to call for me and ask for my help. I needed to enjoy our children at that moment before that moment became the past.

In what ways can we look to the future and help ourselves to enjoy the moments we now have with our children?

Appreciation

Now on his way to Jerusalem, Jesus traveled along the border between Samaria and Galilee. As he was going into a village, ten men who had leprosy met him. They stood at a distance and called out in a loud voice, "Jesus, Master, have pity on us!"

When he saw them, he said, "Go, show yourselves to the priests." And as they went, they were cleansed.

One of them, when he saw he was healed, came back, praising God in a loud voice. He threw himself at Jesus's feet and thanked him—and he was a Samaritan.

Jesus asked, "Were not all ten cleansed? Where are the other nine? Was no one found to return and give praise to God except this foreigner?" Then he said to him, "Rise and go; your faith has made you well."

(Luke 17:11-19—NIV)

Recently I had a call to deliver a calf on a Sunday morning. The calf was dead, and the cow looked bad. I wasn't sure the cow would do well. The people were very appreciative, thanked me for my efforts, paid me, and gave me some vegetables from their garden before I left.

The next day, I had at least three people get upset or impatient with me…"One of those days at the office." One person was upset because the hair on her dog's paws had not been trimmed when it was groomed. No matter what solution we offered, it was declined, and she demanded we do better. We never did offer a solution she considered satisfactory.

I have seen the same kind of situations repeat themselves over the years. People with major problems being appreciative and those with minor problems being inconsiderate. It seems that people who face a daily reality that includes possible loss of life and major economic loss are more considerate and appreciative than those whose daily reality only includes minor problems such as hair trimmed wrong or the wrong color nail polish or bow in the hair.

Personally, I am not very good at showing my appreciation for what other people do for me. After reflecting on my experiences of those two days, I think I'll try harder to show my appreciation.

How well do I show my appreciation? Do I get angry at others over minor problems? How might my actions help or harm the cause of Christ in the lives of people in our community?

Clear, Silent Night

It was 3:15 a.m. when the telephone rang. The man had a cow trying to calve, and she needed help. It is the kind of call I often dread because I miss much needed sleep and have to drive to a place, do demanding work, and then drive back home tired, yet sometimes unable to get back to sleep.

I got out of bed, put on my clothes, walked out through a silent, dark house and through the garage to the car we use to make house calls. On most calls in the middle of the night, my body is weary, and my senses are dull, but this night would be different. I got into the car, pulled onto the road from the driveway, and headed to the farm.

On this night, my senses were particularly keen. The sounds of the car and road were clear. My vision was good, and the stripes and reflectors along the road were sharp and clear. I could see barns and animals in pastures, out the side of the car, due to the full moon. When I arrived the man was standing with the gate open that led to the barn. I stopped the car and got out, and everything was silent except for the man talking to me. The only other sounds were those made by me getting the tools and instruments of calf delivery ready and the splashing of antiseptic and water over them.

The man put a rope on the cow, and I pulled my shirt off and went to work. I determined the position of the calf, put some obstetrical chains on his front legs, manipulated the calf, and then delivered him with the man working the handle on the calf puller. We then hung the calf upside-down on the fence to let fluids drain from his lungs. After that, we laid the calf on the ground, and he began to breathe normally. I gave some medication to the cow, took the rope off, and slapped her on the rump. She got up and began to lick the calf. I then began to clean my equipment and my arms with water from a running water hose.

The night was quiet and still. The night air was cool, and the sky was clear. The moon was full and approximately one third of the way up from the horizon in the western sky. You could see the stars in the sky away from the moon. I was bending over the equipment with the water hose, and I looked over my left shoulder to see the calf pick up his head and shake it. The cow was gently cleaning the calf. I looked to my right to see the back of the call car with equipment boxes stacked on top of one another. Up over the top of the car, in the distance, was the full moon. I finished washing, straightened up, looked back at the cow and calf, then at the car, the sky and the moon, and then looked at the man where he stood in silence. Then I said, "Sometimes people ask me where I work. For tonight, this is where I work." I put my shirt back on, got in the car to leave, and thought to myself again, "Tonight, this is where I work." As I drove back home, my senses were still sharp and keen. At 4:30 a.m., I got back into bed and said a little prayer of thanks to God.

I had just experienced one of the most rewarding things that I do professionally. I had delivered a live calf, and the cow was a good mother taking care of the calf. It happened at an hour when the noise and haste of the day were not present, yet my senses were very keen allowing me to take in all the sights, sounds, odors, and feelings of the moment. When I was finished, I was able to pause, look around, and enjoy seeing the creation of God in the quiet setting of that barn yard.

I have delivered many calves under much worse circumstances and come away tired and weary. That night was different, and the sense of personal accomplishment was great. Can you think of times in your work when your senses were keen, and the personal reward was great? Did you somehow sense the hand of God and see the wonders of his creation?

Strength of a Workhorse

There are show horses, and there are work horses. We all know it, but there are some differences that we don't always think about.

Show horses are slick, shiny, and pretty to look at. They also require a lot of special care, extra energy and time and are put on display and admired by people for their physical form. They are often temperamental and have obnoxious habits as a result of boredom from standing in a stall most of their lives.

Work horses are not as pretty, but their hard muscles are usually well-defined. They do not require a lot of special care and usually have an even disposition. They are calm, easy going, strong, and have little desire for a lot of attention. They know their master, learn discipline, and are eager and willing to take on the duty of daily work for the rest of their lives.

After the first few years of learning discipline, the work horse becomes stronger and more efficient at doing the work set before him. Through his younger and middle years, the work horse accomplishes a great deal and seldom requires anything more than the necessities for daily living. He sets his shoulder to the harness daily, without complaining, and his need for thanks is fulfilled by a pat when the day is finished and the harness is lifted from his shoulder.

In the years when his physical strength starts to decrease, his master will harness him with a strong, young horse to ease his load. During that initial period, he puts forth special effort as an example and as instruction to the younger horse on how he is to serve his master in the years to come. After that initial instruction, he allows the younger horse to assume his full share of the load. Eventually, the old horse is replaced by a young horse, and the horse he taught teaches the new one. He admires the other horses working together and is thankful for the well-deserved rest he now has.

The old horse is admired by others for qualities that have been present throughout his working life, and they realize those qualities are still present even though he no longer goes to the fields to work. The work horse is patient, kind, undemanding, has a sincere heart and doesn't try to make others believe he is something that he is not. Above all, he is loyal and true to those he loves and serves and is a quiet example of courage to all of those around him. When he finally goes to be with his true master, he will reap his full reward and hear the words ring true:

"Well done good and faithful servant…"

"Take my yoke upon you, and learn from me, for I am gentle and humble in heart, and you will find rest for your souls. For my yoke is easy, and my burden is light."

Surprise Packages

A number of years ago, I received a call to go look at a calf for someone. As I drove up to the place, I saw a number of things that let me evaluate the situation. On occasion you will be wrong, but usually you can tell a lot about what you will be dealing with by the surroundings and the nature of the people for whom you are working.

I pulled into the driveway where the trailer house was set on blocks alongside it. Several barking dogs greeted me as I pulled to a stop, and the owner came out of the house. There were numerous rental trailers (like U-Haul trailers) on the place. Some were up on blocks with the wheels off, some were parked in the area behind the trailers on blocks, and one had the wheels back on and looked ready to be used. Grass and weeds had grown up between the trailers outback. There were ten or twelve of them in all.

The man led me through a maze of tires, wheels, and axles to the calf pen. The fence was made of used materials, and there was very little vegetation inside. At one end of the pen there was a low shed, and there was a water trough at the other end, with a feed trough and hay in between. Flies were a problem, but the calves were well-fed and in good health except for the one I was called to see.

The rest of the place where the man lived was covered with old cars, tractors, and other worn out equipment that were good for parts if you had need for them. Grass and weeds had grown up in the spaces between the old equipment.

The man was approximately forty years old and was wearing old clothes which were soiled with bearing grease and material from brakes on the trailer on which he had been working. His beard had not been shaved for two or three days. He spoke slowly with a soft voice. His hands were thick and strong. His fingers were thick, and his fingernails were trimmed short or broken off near the quick with grease and dirt under them. There were small cuts and scrapes all over his hands and fingers which were filled with dirt and grease.

The sick calf had pneumonia. I gave it some medications and left some medicine for him to give over the next several days. It would make a complete recovery.

We walked back to my car so I could write the receipt and he could pay me. I told him the amount, and he began to write his check, using my clipboard, as he was kneeling on the ground beside the car. I could not see what he wrote, but I could tell by his hand motions his writing was slow and deliberate. When he finished, he clipped the check to the clip board, handed it back to me, and I got the surprise of a lifetime. On the check was the most beautiful handwriting I had ever seen. I was shocked. The next time I went to his place, I complimented him and asked if he did any art work. Come to find out, he had explored his artistic talent to some extent and has done several paintings.

I have done work for this man over the years, and he has always been good to work with. I must admit, on the first trip to his place, I made certain judgments about him. His check shocked me back to my senses and caused me to take a good look at him. That was fifteen years ago, and I still marvel at his hand writing every time we get a check from him.

Have you ever noticed how we tend to categorize or judge people? Teachers sometimes have low expectations of a child (based on a test score) even before the first day of school. Employees sometimes base their opinion of the boss on what they have heard from others rather than on their own experiences.

My experience with this man has caused me to take a little more time to evaluate people. In every one, you will find a small surprise if you look closely.

Can you think of any surprise packages? I can think of a couple:

A king who came in the form of a child in a manger.

A missionary worker to Africa who came in the form of a "Surfer."

Survival

The long-term survival of any nation is dependent upon the honesty and moral integrity of each citizen of that nation.

Honesty and moral integrity cannot be legislated or learned at school. They are taught in the home by Godfearing men and women.

Things, Friendship, and Faith

Time turns things into junk. Friendship and faith become more valuable as time passes.

Material things we can possess. Friendship and faith we cannot possess, but we must continually give of ourselves in order to fully appreciate.

Allowing Children to Grow

On several occasions, our children have celebrated their birthdays at my parents' house in the country. We have the kids who are invited to the party come to our house first, and then we go to my parents' house to spend a few hours playing games and cooking hot dogs and hamburgers outside.

It had been raining for a couple of days prior to one party, and rain was predicted for the day of the party. That being the situation, my dad and his helper moved all the equipment out of the middle portion of his largest barn so the kids would have a place to play it if rained.

Shortly after we arrived, it started to rain hard. All the kids loaded into the pickup, and I drove them down to the barn. It was raining so hard they got soaked just running from the truck to the barn. Inside the barn it was noisy from the rain falling on the sheet metal roof. We marked off "four square" on the floor with a chalk line and put up the volleyball net. The kids started to play, and I went back to the house to cook the food. My dad stayed with the kids.

About an hour and a half later, I went back to the barn to get them, and they seemed to really be enjoying themselves. They had been playing volleyball, washer toss, and four square. Back at the house, we ate on the front porch and watched it rain. I was visiting with my dad, and he made a comment about the games they played in the barn. He said, "I don't know all the games they played with the volleyball and net, but I only recognized the first game which was volleyball. They played four other games but they just made them up as they went." After lunch, I went back to the barn with the kids and watched as they made up new games with the washers.

After thinking about it, I am sure I would have insisted the kids play volleyball the "right way" if I had been in the barn with them to start with. They wouldn't have had as much fun, and I would have prevented them from using their natural childhood creativity. As it was, I got to see them make up a couple of new games with the washers because my dad had been with them initially.

My dad has always had good rapport with kids. He knows when to be strict, but he also knows when to back off and allow them to be children and use their natural curiosity and creativity. He always seems to have a good balance when dealing with kids.

That day the kids had fun, my dad enjoyed being with them, and I learned a little bit about dealing with kids. It just shows that every person has a role to play. People of all ages need one another. At times people of one generation try to tell the next generation what they are doing wrong. It often leads to rebellion and resentment. A quiet, but firm example seems to be a better teacher and allows the younger people to openly or privately acknowledge: "So that's how you do it." or "That's what he has been trying to show me."

We can all look to the master teacher by reading our Bibles and seeing how Jesus taught by example. Let us all pray that we can learn from one another, as we are guided by God, through the Bible.

Listening

Pigs and needles don't mix. Anyone who has helped restrain a 150 pound pig for an injection knows what a wrestling match it can be. A number of years ago, I went out to remove sutures from a sow that weighed approximately 300 pounds. Ten days earlier, my associate had done a C-section on the sow. He had left a bottle of antibiotics for a fourteen year old boy to give injections to the sow daily. I jokingly asked the young man if he had any trouble with the injections. He answered, "No," and I laughed at him. At that point, I started to go about my work, but for some reason I turned back to him and asked about it again. He stuck with his story that he had no trouble giving injections to this 300 pound sow all by himself. He told me he put an ice cube on the injection site until it melted, and then he put the needle in and the sow didn't feel it.

I had been through five years of college and had been in practice for five years, and this fourteen year old young man had just taught me something about veterinary medicine. Had I not listened to him for a few minutes, I would not have learned from him. As it is, I have a technique I use periodically.

Most of us will sit in front of a TV for thirty or forty minutes without saying a word. We will listen, not get up from our seat, or interrupt the program by diverting our attention to a book or to talk to someone else in the room. We do this even though we know that some of what is said on the TV may not be true or accurate.

I know we all have teenage kids who would like to talk to their parents without being interrupted, having their parents shake their heads or roll their eyes. If one of our children came into the room where we were watching TV, turned it off, sat down on the couch and said, "I want to talk to you," would we willingly and patiently listen? Would we be able to hear them out, without interruption, even though some of what they said may be inaccurate? I hope we would. We might learn something about our children, and we might learn something about ourselves. They need to learn from us, and we need to learn from them. It is a two-way street. Children and parents need to listen and talk without either one dominating the conversation. Ideally there should be periods of silence when each is listening to his or her own heart. Solutions are often reached during silent reflection.

Somehow, we need to come to understand that children of all ages need their parents and parents of all ages need their children. We need to put aside the myth that we perpetuate in our society—that when children become teenagers, they think they know it all, and parents who have teenagers are out of step with the times. Neither one is true. Daily interaction with our children that is not tense or angry is necessary if we are to do our job in the home. That kind of interaction is only possible when there is cooperation from both sides. May we all pray to God for guidance in raising our children.

Beautiful Living

I received a call late one evening to deliver a calf. The client had a few cows, and I had never been to her place before. She gave me directions, and I drove through the dark countryside to her place. By the time I arrived, the cow had already given birth but still needed to be examined. The cow was in a chute, and the lady had put a light over the chute and run an extension cord from the barn so I would not have to work by flashlight. The lady was apologetic for having called me at night, and she spoke in a courteous manner. After I examined the cow, the lady had a bucket of water, soap, and rags for me to clean with. Then she handed me a towel to dry with after I had washed.

Six weeks later, she called again and had another cow with difficulty calving. This time it was the middle of the day, and I was able to see her house; the barn, cattle pens, and the cow she had already put in the chute. We put a rope on the cow's horns and turned her out into a small pen, and then I went to work. The lady was very helpful and tied the rope off when I needed, handed the bucket to me with my instruments in it and had another bucket with fresh water in case I needed it. The lady held the cow's tail out of my way; I repositioned the calf and put obstetrical chains on its legs. The lady then got the calf puller for me, and we delivered a live calf. I hung the calf over the top board of the fence to allow fluids to drain from its lungs and then put it back on the ground. I then gave some medication to the cow, the lady and I removed the equipment from the pen, and I removed the rope from the cow. The cow started to take care of the calf.

The lady and I paused to look at the newborn calf as the cow licked it, and then we went to clean the equipment in water from a hose. I washed the equipment and my hands and arms with soap she had provided and dried with a clean towel she had ready. We then walked back out to the pen to take one last look at the cow and calf.

In the large pen in the barnyard were small piles of hay the lady had put out earlier. She had carried the bales of hay herself and then arranged the hay in the small piles that morning. There was one pile of hay for each of her cows. The lady lived on an old place, but the pens were in a good state of repair. There was a small pile of old tires and broken equipment parts between the pens and a small single car garage where she kept her car. The fence around the house was old but well kept. The modest frame house had wooden siding that was painted white with black trim. The lady was pleasant to visit with, and I spent an extra few minutes talking with her. She was dressed in overalls and a long sleeved shirt and had on work shoes. She had been outside most of the morning, but you could tell she had fixed her hair and dressed appropriately for her morning work. During our conversation, I found out she was seventy-three years old.

The lady also told me she was born on that place, about leaving home, marrying, and eventually coming back with her husband to live there. She spoke of the death of her parents, losing her husband, working the land, selling part of the land, widening of the road which put the house closer to the road and many other things. During our conversation, she spoke of the past, talked about living in the present and looked forward to the future, all without complaining about the present problems, voicing regret of things in the past or expressing fears about the future.

We said good-bye to one another, and I got in my car and drove to the road. I had just been given a tremendous boost by her example of living daily with a good attitude and a beautiful spirit. I pray to God that if I am allowed to stay on this earth as long as she, I will be able to cultivate her beautiful spirit in my own life.

The Mare In The Trough

I was going on a call to vaccinate a group of heifers for brucellosis (a disease which causes abortions in cattle). I had made the appointment two days earlier with one of the hands who worked on the ranch. I got off the interstate highway, drove down a rough county road, over a wooden bridge, up over the crest of a hill and then made a ninety degree turn where the road changed from black top to caliche, beginning my descent into the Nueces River bottom. In my rear view mirror, I could see the clouds of caliche dust billow up in the disturbed air behind the car. At the entrance to the ranch, I stopped, opened the gate, drove through, and then closed the gate behind me. I pulled up just as the ranch hands finished herding the cattle into the pens.

It was the middle of an afternoon in August, and the sun was beating down. Dust rose from the pens where the cattle walked around, and the horses were lathered up with sweat from working the cattle. There was not a breath of wind, and I began to sweat. The cowboys got off the horses, loosened the girth cinch on the saddles, and then turned the horses loose in the holding pen with the cattle.

After we had been working cattle for a few minutes, I looked up and saw one of the horses standing in a large water trough. The trough was approximately two feet deep and twenty feet in diameter. It was divided in half by a fence so cattle could water from two different pens. The mare laid down in the water trough to cool off, and when she attempted to get back up, the saddle horn caught on the fence running across the middle of the trough. As the mare began to struggle, I told the cowboys they needed to get the mare out of the trough. They turned around to look and laughed at the mare. After a few attempts to rise and being held down by the fence each time, the mare's head went under water, and I saw bubbles start to come up. I ran over to the trough and held the mare's nose above water so she could breathe, and the cowboys managed to loosen the girth strap and take the saddle off. The mare was then able to struggle to her feet.

The cowboys had not realized the mare was really in trouble until I ran to the trough and held her nose out of the water. We got the mare out of the trough, and then she stood there and drank a lot of water while we went back to working the cattle. By the time we had finished working the cattle, the mare had colic from drinking too much water. I then had to treat her for colic.

A few questions about the situation:

Are we sometimes drawn to things that seem very inviting and refreshing when we are tired or exhausted?

When we are drawn to such things, while exhausted, do we tend to want to get right into the middle of it and even immerse ourselves in it?

Do we fail to see the hazards that are present and fail to take into consideration the burdens we bear when we are drawn into such things?

When we are in trouble, struggling, and nearly to the point of drowning, do the ones who are closest to us sometimes fail to realize we are in trouble?

When someone finally realizes we are in trouble and is able to save us from the situation, do we sometimes return immediately to it and end up in trouble again?

There was nothing wrong with the tired, hot, sweaty mare getting a drink of water to refresh herself. It was when she tried to get total, immediate relief that she got into trouble. Let us be reminded that when we are tired to the point of exhaustion, we need to be cautious about the hazards that may be present if we seek total, immediate relief. If we get into trouble and someone has to save us from drowning, let us be wise enough to stay away from that situation for a period of time to avoid getting back into trouble.

Full Circle

When a child is born into this world, God has given a gift to the parents from heaven. At first, the infant is held and nurtured in the arms of his mother. After a short while, there are tiny footsteps that walk in circles around the feet of the mother and father. Before long, those footsteps walk along-side the footsteps of a parent and periodically, you see only the steps of the parent when the child is tired of walking and holds his arms upward and says, "Hold you." A little further along the path of life, the child's footsteps are constantly next to the parents, but never more than arm's length from the parent. Eventually, the footsteps are more than arm's length from the steps of the parents, and when the child leaves home, the footsteps are far from the footsteps of the parents.

At times, the paths of the child and the parent are very close, usually when there is a marriage, a birth, severe illness, tragedy or death. The paths of the child and the parent are far apart at times but often come closer together as the parents age. When the parents die, you see only the footsteps of the child. You see the footsteps of the child throughout adult life and on into old age. This life is lived and often a child is born and you see two sets of footsteps again, but the same pattern repeats itself.

As an individual becomes old or physically feeble, he can look over and see that there are footsteps a distance away where once his parents walked. He walks closer and walks a short distance from that path and eventually moves even closer to reach up and hold onto the hand extended down to him. As the end of life on this earth nears, you can see the footsteps of the individual walking small circles around larger footsteps. When death finally comes, there are no longer two sets of footsteps, but one. The heavenly Father has finally picked the child up in his arms and carried him to his journey's end. Once again the child is held in warm, secure, loving arms, the arms of the one who allowed him to live on this earth for a few short years. Life has gone full circle: From the loving arms of God, to the loving arms of parents, through childhood, adulthood, and finally back to the loving arms of God. May we never lose sight of God during our journey.

May 14, 1994

Today, the evening sky was turning from dark grey to black as I drove along the road toward home. As I turned down our street, the first raindrops were starting to fall. I stopped to see if a neighbor needed help to cover materials where he was building a new house. As I pulled into our driveway, the rain began to fall hard. I pulled into the garage, took a few things into the house and then looked for the newspaper. I found the paper and then looked out the window. The rest of my family was not home yet. I never picked the paper up but went out onto the porch and watched it rain.

Within the span of twenty minutes, I saw the rain come straight down without enough wind to move the leaves on the Mesquite trees; I saw rain drip off the roof, form puddles, and start to drain across the yard; I saw the trees sway as the wind blew hard from several directions, and I even saw some hail. I saw streaks of lightning and heard a lot of thunder and the sound of wind. The rest of my family came home, and we went inside the house. Within forty-five minutes, the rain stopped, and the sun began to shine. The grass in the yard seemed to be more intense green than it had been an hour before. We went out on the porch and saw a double rainbow. The one on the bottom was very bright with the one on top being faint.

In less than two hours, I had witnessed the power and beauty of God's creation. The newspaper, the refrigerator, and the TV were all there, but I stepped out onto the porch instead. I think I made the right choice this rainy evening.

In what simple ways can we enjoy God's creation in our daily lives?

Shadows

I often travel small farm roads and county roads after dark. There are sometimes hazards along the way, such as construction that is not well marked, sudden changes from hard surface to caliche road surfaces, ruts or holes in the road. Most of them are not so severe that they would cause you to lose control of your car, but they can scare you at night.

A few days ago I was called, after dark, to check on a horse that I had seen six weeks earlier. I remembered that one section of the road was full of holes and had one low spot that ran all the way across it and would really bounce the car around when hit. There was also a rough spot in a low water crossing, but it was easy enough to steer around in daylight. After dark, you can watch the shadows on the surface of the road where your headlights shine. The shadows of small dips or holes will disappear as you get closer to them, but the shadows of the larger ones don't. I've been watching shadows on the road at night for quite a few years now. They do help you to avoid a lot of jarring bumps or at least allow you to be prepared to get bounced around when you cannot slow down or steer around a bump.

Coming back from that call the other night, I was watching the road surface, and when I got to smoother road, I was thinking. I thought how good it would be if I could learn to read the shadows along life's road as well as I could interpret the shadows along those small county roads.

How can we learn to spot the shadows along the road of life and learn when to slow down, steer around them or know when to hold on tight when we are getting ready to be bounced around by one of life's hazards?

Responsibility

There are a lot of problems in our society today, and there are a lot of explanations put forth as to the cause of those problems.

Very basically:

Boys have not become mature men.

Girls have not become mature women.

Hearers of the Word have not become believers.

Believers have not lived their daily lives according to God's plan and have not become good examples. Therefore, they have not become effective spreaders of the Word.

What can we do, individually, to live more responsibly, and become what God wants us to be?

How Do We Treat Others?

(Mark 9:38-41)

"Teacher," said John, "we saw a man driving out demons in your name, and we told him to stop, because he was not one of us."

"Do not stop him," Jesus said. "No one who does a miracle in my name can in the next moment say anything bad about me, for whoever is not against us is for us. I tell you the truth, anyone who gives you a cup of water in my name because you belong to Christ will certainly not lose his reward." (NIV)

In the above passage do we see ourselves? Do we also see some of the people with whom we associate daily? If so, how do we treat those people?

What's in a Can of Beans?

What's in a can of beans? Beans of course, and a little bit of water…food to nourish the human body. Take a closer look, with your mind, and see what else might be in the can.

Can you see the fertile soil, the earth from which man was formed? Are you able to see the blue skies and the sun that warmed the earth to make the seed sprout? Can you see the green plant and smell the moist, rich soil? Can you see the great billowing thunder clouds, the streaks of lightning, hear the thunder and feel the cool, crisp drops of rain as they fall? When the storm is over, can you see the rainbow painted across the sky when the sun begins to peek through the clouds which had turned the day into night? Can you sense the power and the love of God who created all of those things for you to see, and through it all provided man with the things he needs?

When we give a can of beans to someone from the church pantry, it may be that all they see are beans and water. If it is given with the love and the spirit of Jesus, it may be that the people who received it will someday come to see God and all his creation through that one small gesture of generosity. When we give food, we are really giving a small portion of the love of God to someone.

It is easy to forget, but when we are in the store, may we remember to get a few small items for the church pantry, for…"it is in giving that we receive."

Cooperation

One day, I went to a ranch to work some cows. The ranch hands had rounded the cattle up into the pens early that morning, and they were just getting off the horses when I arrived. The men took the horses over to a small cluster of Mesquite trees and tied the reins on each horse to the branches of the trees. We worked the cattle in a nearby set of pens for the next four or five hours. We finished working about noon.

We then sat down and ate our lunches. After lunch we were to go to another set of pens on the ranch to work another group of cows. The boss told the men to hitch the squeeze chute to one pickup. After that, the men loaded their horses into a trailer hitched behind another pickup that was approximately forty feet from where the horses were tied to the trees. The way the men loaded the horses was unusual compared to the way I have seen a lot of horses loaded into trailers, but routine for the horses on that ranch.

The first man untied the reins from the tree, led the horse over to the back of the trailer, put the reins up over the neck of the horse, patted it on the rear, and it got into the trailer.

The second man untied the reins from the tree, put the reins up over the neck of the horse, led the horse by the bridle over to the back of the trailer, and the horse walked into the trailer.

The third man untied the reins from the tree, put the reins up over the neck of the horse, led the horse to within fifteen feet of the trailer and stopped and the horse continued walking and got into the trailer.

The fourth man untied the reins from the tree, put the reins up over the neck of the horse, stood beside the horse without touching him and started walking toward the trailer. The horse followed. The man stopped walking about halfway to the trailer, and the horse continued walking and stepped up into the trailer. The man then closed the trailer gate behind the last two horses.

I have seen quite a few horses loaded into trailers, but never anything quite like that. I have seen it take several minutes or even an hour to load a single horse into a trailer. I saw a lady try to load a horse for nearly an hour one time and then finally give up and walk the horse home, along-side the road, over a mile away. She then caught a ride back to get her pickup and trailer. I have put stitches in horses to close wounds caused when the horse had become fractious when the owner was attempting to load it into a trailer.

On the job, in the home, and at church, do we willingly cooperate with one another and accomplish the task at hand without unnecessary conflict? Do we sometimes cause others a lot of frustration and at the same time inflict wounds on ourselves because we don't cooperate?

Standing Before The Cross

Fourscore and seven years ago, our fathers brought forth upon this continent a new nation, conceived in liberty, and dedicated to the proposition that all men are created equal.

Now we are engaged in a great civil war, testing whether that nation—or any nation, so conceived and so dedicated—can long endure.

We are met on a great battlefield of that war. We are met to dedicate a portion of it as the final resting place of those who have given their lives that that nation might live.

It is altogether fitting and proper that we should do this.

But, in a larger sense, we cannot dedicate, we cannot consecrate, we cannot hallow, this ground. The brave men, living and dead, who struggled here, have consecrated it, far above our power to add or to detract.

The world will very little note nor long remember what we say here; but it can never forget what they did here.

It is for us, the living, rather, to be dedicated, here, to the unfinished work that they have thus far so nobly carried on. It is rather for us to be here dedicated to the great task remaining before us; that from these honored dead we take increased devotion to that cause for which they here gave the last full measure of devotion; that we here highly resolve that these dead shall not have died in vain; that the nation shall, under God, have a new birth of freedom, and that government of the people, by the people, for the people, shall not perish from the earth.

Abraham Lincoln
Gettysburg, Pennsylvania
November 19, 1863

In a spiritual sense, when we stand before the cross…"we cannot consecrate, we cannot hallow, this ground"…on which the cross stands. Christ has…"consecrated it, far above our power to add or to detract." "The world will very little note nor long remember what we say here;" (when we are facing the cross) but the world cannot forget what Christ did there.

When facing the cross, "It is rather for us to be here dedicated to the great task remaining before us;" May we…"take increased devotion to that cause for which…"He"…gave the last full measure of devotion."

Special Days and Friends

God gives us special days. He also gives each one of us special friends. Every once in a great while he allows us to spend one of those days with one of those special friends.

Think back to one of those days you spent with a special friend. Remember the lift it gave to your spirit and the joy and appreciation you felt in your heart. Then thank God for the special days and special friends in your life.

Christmas

During this holiday season, it is my hope that we could all focus on the spirit of the Christ Child.

May we come to understand that it is only through giving that we can receive and fully understand the love of the Father who sent His Son into the world for all of us.

Things

We have just finished a time of celebration. For a great number of people, it has been a special time for focusing on the coming of Christ into the world. For others it is nothing more than a time of celebration that involves food and a lot of material gifts. Throughout most of it, people get together with family and friends.

In our society, we exchange a lot of gifts. Some of the things are given for a specific purpose, but a lot of things are given out of guilt or obligation and are soon forgotten. As a matter of fact, a lot of gifts are given along with the receipt, so people can take the gift back if it doesn't fit or if they just do not like the gift. We spend a lot of time and go to a lot of trouble to make some feeble attempt at showing our generosity or trying to show someone we love them.

Things have a place in all of our lives. We can all think back and remember a gift we received as a child, or something that was given to us by someone special or that we received on a special occasion. Most of the things we opened last month are already forgotten. Things meaning the most to us are things that remind us of special people or special events in our lives.

The other day, I used a hammer to drive some nails, and then I needed to measure a lot of spaces at eleven inches. I picked up the hammer and looked at the handle which had three notches in it. One of the notches was eleven inches from the head of the hammer. I used it instead of a tape measure. Those notches in the hammer handle took me back a lot of years. As a young boy, I remember standing beside a fence with only the top strand of barbed wire stapled to the posts. My dad did a little figuring about how he wanted the other four wires spaced on the fence, and then he used his pocket knife to carve the notches into the handle of the hammer. When we had a fence to build, we used that hammer to be sure the wires were spaced properly. For me, that hammer and the notches in the handle have special meaning.

In the corner of our dining room sits an old oak high chair. It has no particular value as an antique. It is missing the tray, is rather plain, and has no ornate carving on it. When I look at it, it reminds me of my mother and her brothers and sisters because they all sat in it as infants. It also reminds me of my grandmother. She was a small woman, and she used to sit in that chair and peel potatoes when she was in the kitchen. I only saw her six or eight times in my life, but I can still see her sitting in that chair.

On top of a kitchen cabinet, and in the cabinet, are a kerosene lamp, a straight razor with a note and leather case and sickles used to trim grass. They all remind me of my grandmother and grandfather who I only had opportunity to see a few times during my life. There are special things about those items that remind me of their special qualities and character.

The things that bring back the most memories for me have very little monetary value. It is the people or the events that they remind me of that makes them of some value to me.

There is one more thing that is special to me. It reminds me of a special time in history and something that was done for me and a lot of others. In the church where I grew up, there were stained glass windows at the front of the building. There was also a cross.

The cross on which Jesus hung was a cruel instrument of death. I'm sure it was rather plain and had no significant monetary value. The love that was shown there is of more value than anyone can express. A gift was given there which has no particular monetary value because it is of such great worth.

When the community in which I was raised grew, so did the church family. The people eventually decided to build a new building in which to meet. It had no stained glass windows, but it still had a cross. There was a short aisle which led form the double doors at the main entrance to the seating area. Right in the middle of that aisle was a stone cross. The cross was large. I could walk under the cross piece. It was placed there so people would be reminded of what Jesus did on the cross as they entered the building and as they departed.

May we never fail to remember the cross and what happened there. May we be constantly reminded of the love of the Father and the gift of the Son when we see or think about the cross.

New Beginnings
(March 21, 1995)

Today, I was on the road making house calls. When driving, I usually use the time to think or observe the countryside as I drive along the road. I made two trips to Sandia today.

Today, I noticed a few things that I see every spring, but they seemed to be more vivid this time, because I drove the same roads both in the morning and in the afternoon.

Along the fence lines and in the pastures, I saw the golden yellow color of the Huisache trees in full bloom. The Hackberry trees were light green in color due to their young tender leaves. Still lighter green were the new wispy leaves of the Mesquite trees. Some underbrush had a bloom that was pale yellow.

On a hillside pasture, cows were grazing the new green grass that was mixed with the dry brown grass of winter. In cultivated fields, I saw young corn that was pale green in color.

All of these things are just the beginning. Soon, the blooms will fall off, and the leaves will become darker green as they mature. The tenderness and immaturity of the new leaves will be changed to stronger adult leaves. The pastures will soon be solid green without the mixture of brown and green grass, and the fields of corn will be the dark green color of growing plants. Eventually, all of the plants will come to full maturity, produce fruit, and die, or the leaves will die and fall to the ground.

We often compare these things in nature to life as a whole. I believe God shows us these things in nature on a yearly basis to allow us to have a renewal of our spirits. We can have new beginnings at any time in our lives, and this annual renewal in nature allows us to have the courage to start new things during different parts of our lives. Also, by seeing the annual cycle and continual renewal in nature, we can come to fully understand the beauty of the different stages of our lives.

Judging Others

I had just finished putting the last stitch in the lamb's head and gone back to the car to get it a shot of antibiotics. It would prove to be the first of four times we would suture this lamb in a five month period of time. As I was walking back to the barn, a pickup with three young men pulled up and came to a sudden halt. One of the young men jumped out of the pickup and rushed over to where I was working on the lamb. He said he had a dog with a gunshot wound. I told him I would come look after I gave the lamb a shot. I gave the injection and then walked over to the pickup. One young man had been riding in the back of the pickup with a large Labrador Retriever, and he was holding his hand over a hole in the dog's left side.

I guessed the three young men to be twenty to twenty-five years of age. They had been out bird hunting and were all wearing leg protectors to prevent snake bite. They had their vests, ammunition, and guns in the pickup. I looked at the dog quickly and listened to its heart and lungs and determined it was in shock. I had the young man lift his hand from the dog's side, and I saw the single hole with blood flowing from it. I gave the dog an intravenous injection to help reduce shock, and then I told the men to head to the clinic. As I turned to walk away, I saw a beer can in an insulated can holder in the back of the truck.

As I walked back to my car, I was thinking about the beer can and wondering why people couldn't learn that alcohol and most other activities don't mix. During the short drive to the clinic, I wondered out loud why people use alcohol in dangerous situations, or why they use alcohol at all. I got angry about the situation and was ready to lecture the young men and blame them for the injury to the dog. Once we got to the clinic I forgot about that, and we took the dog straight to the surgery room, leaving a trail of blood as we went.

I placed an IV catheter in the dog and began to give IV fluids as rapidly as possible. I talked with the owner of the dog and told him that we have a very poor outlook and recommended that we do surgery even though the risk was extremely high. He gave approval, and I had them assist me where possible. After putting the dog on the anesthetic machine, I did a surgical prep and began surgery. It didn't take long to discover numerous perforations in the intestinal tract of the dog and injury to other abdominal organs. I stopped and talked with the owner of the dog, gave him an extremely poor outlook and discussed with him what kind of recovery we would have if the dog survived. He elected to put the dog to sleep. At that point, the young man who had shot the dog broke down and cried. Before they left, the owner of the dog and the other young man offered to clean up the clinic, but I told them I would do it. As they left, I told them I was sorry about the loss of the dog, but I felt they had made the right decision. At that point I was still thinking about the alcohol and wondering what I could have said to make an impression on those young men. As it was, I had held my tongue and been sympathetic with them about the loss of the dog.

I spent the next hour and a half cleaning surgery instruments, the surgery room, mopping floors and cleaning the sidewalk where we had left a trail of blood. During that time, I reflected on what had happened over the last two hours and what I could have done differently. In regard to the dog, I would have done the same thing. With the young men? Could I have said something that would have been better for them besides giving them the best advice I could, being sympathetic and holding my tongue?

The young men told me they had finished their bird hunt and then started to sight in their rifle for use in the upcoming deer season. The dog had gotten loose, and just as the one man was shooting, the dog ran into the path of the bullet. What had I seen that angered me earlier? I had seen one beer can in an insulated can holder in the back of a pickup. I had seen into the front of the pickup and the entire bed of the pickup, and that was all I had seen. I had also worked with those three young men for over an hour and stood within two feet of all three of them.

Had I smelled even a faint odor of alcohol...? No.

Did they make judgments that seemed irrational, or did they use any language that indicated their tongues had been loosened by the effects of alcohol...? No.

I had seen something, made a quick judgment and become angry. The situation at hand had involved some time during which the anger had been put aside for a period of time, and I had become sympathetic with the people over the loss of the dog. After that, I had some time alone to think. I determined in my own mind that alcohol was probably not involved at all. My initial judgment and anger had been wrong, and fortunately, I had held my tongue. I learned something that day about making quick judgments, anger, and controlling my tongue. What would have been the impact on those three young men if I had spoken while I was angry?

Solitude

It was green, black, and yellow. It was noisy and stirred up a lot of dust as it rolled in the dirt. Parts of it were too hot to touch. Inside it was cool and quiet, and for me, a place of solitude.

What I just described is a John Deere tractor. Yes, it has an AM/FM radio, but I do not turn it on. Just hearing the sounds of the machine is enough for me. Fortunately I have a friend who farms, so I can drive a tractor when they are working in the fields.

Most people would ask how in the world that could be a place of solitude. For me it is. When on a tractor, I am alone, relaxed, and free to think about where I'm going and where I've been. My mind is free to find answers to problems that don't seem to have an answer when I confront them during my normal daily work. I am also free to think about my relationship with God and find a great deal of satisfaction and comfort in working the ground He said we would. I am reminded that God made us from the earth and that we will return to the earth. I am also reminded of how dependent we are on the earth for our daily survival.

At the end of the day, I am tired (a good kind of tired). I can look back at what I have done and look forward to returning home to my family. I usually see a beautiful, unobstructed sunset also.

Where is your place of solitude? What are your feelings after a restful cleansing of your mind and an honest opening of your heart to God?

April 23, 1995

A week ago today, I was at my parents' place, and I did something I usually do on Easter Sunday. I walked through a couple of gates that lead past the corral and a small hay barn and down the gentle slope in the small fenced area down below the barn. I walked through the gate at the far end of the pen and stopped to check the fruit on a Mulberry tree that grows on a bluff behind the barn and separates the barn from a small pasture below. The berries were not quite ripe, but I ate one or two that were almost ripe anyway. I also checked a couple more trees further up the dry creek bed at the base of the bluff.

Yesterday (April 22), Sheri and the girls and I were at Papalote again. Kristen and I went out for a driving lesson around a pasture we call "The Willie Long Patch," named after the man from whom my dad purchased the land. We drove grandpa's old pickup. After the driving was over, Kristen and I went back into the house, and in a minute Melany and Sheri came walking into the house. They had purple fingers, lips, and tongues. I knew where they had been.

Today (April 23), while Melany was riding Red, a horse she and Kristen bought, Kristen and I walked down to the Mulberry trees and ate the fresh, sweet fruit from the trees. After Melany had finished riding Red, and Kristen started to ride, Melany and I went down to the trees and ate berries again. All of us ended up with purple fingers, lips, and tongues.

When I was a boy, and my dad and I went to Papalote, Paul Miller—who lived down the road—would usually come riding up on their tractor soon after we arrived. If we didn't have any work that was pressing, my dad would let me go with Paul, and we would often go fishing or squirrel hunting. The tractor was our transportation. One spring, Paul and I rode up to their house on the tractor, and his mother came out and handed us an empty bowl. The mulberries were ripe, and she wanted enough to make a pie. Paul and I drove under the trees on the tractor and stood on the tractor and picked mulberries. As soon as we got the bowl full, we began to eat berries until we were full. They were so sweet. I guess that is what got me started on mulberries. I may have eaten them prior to that, but driving from tree to tree and picking and eating mulberries from the tractor is still a vivid memory from my growing-up years.

I guess our girls first ate mulberries when I picked them and handed them down to small, waiting hands. Soon I had to hold the girls up on my shoulders so they could pick them and eat them without the berries ever being touched by other hands. I taught them that the sweetest ripe berries were the darkest ones. Now the girls are big enough to stand on the ground and pick the berries for themselves. Every once in a while, dad is needed to pull a higher branch down so the girls can reach some dark, ripe berries.

A cool front blew through last evening, and this morning it was chilly and overcast. By late in the afternoon when the girls and I were a Papalote, the sun had broken through, and the air was cool and crisp. After we had gotten into the pickup and said goodbye to grandma and grandpa, we headed down the driveway. As we turned onto the road, we looked to the western sky and saw the sun's rays radiating down through the clouds which had hidden the sun. About half an hour later we saw the brilliant orange color of the sun on the horizon as we turned onto Farm Road 624 and headed toward our house.

This afternoon, we had truly tasted the bounty and seen the beauty of the creation of God.

In thinking about the purple fingers, lips, and tongues, and of the girls and myself, I came to the realization that a part of my childhood had become a part of their childhood. The thought made me smile.

Monday morning, I had to clean the last of the purple stain from under my fingernails when I got to work. The events of the previous afternoon came sharply into focus again. I hope that the victory of Christ and the joy of purple fingers, purple lips, and purple tongues at Easter time will be passed from generation to generation in our family.

Men's Retreat

Scriptures: Selected excerpts from the third and fourth chapters of Philippians (NIV).

I want to know Christ and the power of his resurrection and the fellowship of sharing in his sufferings, becoming like him in his death, and so, somehow, to attain to the resurrection from the dead.
Brothers, I do not consider myself yet to have taken hold of it. But one thing I do: Forgetting what is behind and straining toward what is ahead, I press on toward the goal to win the prize for which God has called me heavenward in Christ Jesus.
Finally, brothers, whatever is true, whatever is noble, whatever is right, whatever is pure, whatever is lovely, whatever is admirable—if anything is excellent or praiseworthy—think about such things. Whatever you have learned or received or heard from me, or seen in me—put it into practice. And the God of peace will be with you.

Last month some men of the congregation went on a retreat that lasted less than twenty-four hours. We slept very little and ate a lot. We sang, prayed, listened to good speakers, and discussed many topics.
We talked about our country, God, church, our wives, our children, and work. We discussed and made commitments about our personal relationships and responsibilities in all of those areas.
We came to more fully understand that we cannot change the past, but we must learn from it. We have no desire to go back to the past. It is our hope and prayer, for our country and our families, that our next step into the future will be a step up instead of another step down. Please pray for all of us.
Thanks to our families for allowing us to have that time together.

Scratching For Seed
(March 28, 1995)

Today, I went to visit a friend of mine who is a farmer. When I go to visit, we usually ride around in his pickup checking on the crops, or tractors, if they are in the fields. We usually eat lunch together.

Prior to the planting season, they check the planters over to be sure they are in good working order for the short but intensive time they are in the fields planting the seed. They select the proper gears and even put seed in the planter boxes and turn the drive wheels of the planter. They catch the seed and count to be sure the correct number of seeds will be planted in a given distance.

Once they go to the fields, they plant a short distance and then stop the tractor and get a knife or sharp stick and dig where the planter just put seed in the ground. They commonly call this "scratching" for seed. They check the depth to make sure the seeds are in moist dirt with the proper amount of dirt covering them. They also check the spacing between the seeds so the mature plants will have enough room and moisture to produce good crops.

Today, David and I spent a lot of time on our knees scratching for seed. It was the first day the planters were back in the fields after some rain so adjustments had to be made. The moisture levels and the texture of the soil were different from the last time they had planted prior to the rain. David even made adjustments to one planter after it moved from one field to another.

Over the years, I saw David and his dad on their knees a number of times. I have helped scratch for seed a few times, too. It takes time and you get dirty from being on your hands and knees digging in the soil. David's dad died last year. When David and I were in the field today, David talked about what Papa Frank said the last few times he checked the seed. Papa Frank lived to be eighty-four, and when he would get down on his knees to scratch for seed, the first thing he would do is put his hands together in prayer. David would ask him if he was praying that the seed would come up, and his reply was that he was praying *he* could get back up! Papa Frank had quite a sense of humor.

In the Bible, we read about the sowing of seed compared to spreading the word of God. My questions is: Do we ever stop to check to see if we are effective in how we place the seed in the fertile soil of the lives of other people? Maybe every once in a while we should get down on our knees, get a little dirty, and spend some time scratching for seed.

Frustration

A number of years ago, I received a call to go check someone's family milk cow. At the time I had a practice limited to house calls, and I was operating out of the back of a 1974 Ford Pinto. From my house in Corpus Christi, I drove north on Interstate 37 to the small community of Edroy, Texas, exited on a Farm-to-Market road, and drove through the middle of the small town. I drove past the post office, tractor dealership, grain elevator, cotton gin, and a feedlot on the edge of town. I drove approximately one mile outside of town and turned into the driveway where I was to look at the cow. It was an old farm house with a few sheds and a set of pens. As I pulled to a stop, the man and his young son walked out of the house across the yard and over to the pens where I was parked.

There had been a lot of rain recently, so the ground was wet and the pens were ankle deep in mud where livestock had been going to feed. The cow was in a pen, but there was not a chute. I did not think it would be a problem because she was gentle. The pen she was in had a post in the center that was the support for a lean-to shed that came off a larger shed. The fence was tall with horizontal boards and had a mesh wire tacked to it down low. On the outside of the fence, they had attached white picket fence for decoration. The owner put a rope on the cow and took a wrap around the post in the center of the pen. Outside the pen, his young son picked up a stick and began to walk back and forth, hitting the picket fence. He yelled for his dog, and a big German Shepherd came and began walking beside him and barked loudly and constantly as the boy rattled the stick along the picket fence.

As I began to attempt to take the temperature of the cow, a horse chased five heifers into the pen next to the one where we were working, crowded them into the corner, and then as the heifers ran out of the pen, the horse would spin, kick the fence that divided the two pens, and throw mud on me, the owner, and the milk cow. This happened four or five times over the next few minutes.

I was holding the cow's tail and attempting to insert the thermometer as she circled around the post in the center of the pen. The man had only taken a wrap around the post with the rope, so he was also walking a circle around the post to keep the cow from getting loose. All three of us were ankle deep in mud.

After approximately ten minutes of wasted time and motion, and frustration rising fast, I had enough. Finally, I stopped and shouted at the man, above the noise of the dog and the boy, "Wait a minute! You whip that boy and take him to the house, I'll whip that dog and put him in the shed, and then maybe we can get something done!" The man stopped, stared at me, and didn't say a word. He then turned and climbed over the fence, whipped the boy, and headed to the house. I climbed over the fence, grabbed the dog by the collar, and locked him in the shed. I also closed the gate to the pen next to us to keep the horse and the heifers out.

The man and I climbed back into the pen at about the same time. He tied the cow back to the post in the center of the pen, the cow stood still, and I was taking her temperature. Neither the man nor I had said a word since I yelled at him. I was a little embarrassed at having told him to whip his boy, but since he had, I was obligated to do what I had done to the dog. We stood there in silence as the thermometer registered. Finally the man spoke and said, "We should have done that a long time ago!"

The cow had mastitis, and I treated her and left medication for him to use. He paid me and thanked me. As I drove away, the boy was still in the house and the dog was still in the shed.

Tears of the Old Horse

I have a friend who farms and ranches with his brother. They have a lot of cows, so they keep horses on the ranch to work them. There were a couple of old horses that had been on the place a long time. When the bay mare and the grey gelding got too old to work cattle, they were moved to a small pasture close to the shop where they could be checked daily and fed grain and hay as needed.

The bay mare died a couple of years ago.

The old gelding was between thirty and thirty-five years old and had been blind in one eye for a lot of years. When he was younger, he was still good to ride even though he had the one bad eye. As with most old horses, the gelding would lose weight through the winter months and then gain it back during the spring and summer months when there was lush grass. In the spring, he would also shed his winter coat and get a slick, new coat of hair.

A couple of weeks ago, I was over at their ranch three days in a row. As Frank and I drove past the small pasture where the horse was grazing, he commented to me that this year the old horse had not gained weight, and it had not grown a new, slick hair coat as in years past. We discussed the possible causes, and then Frank asked me, "What happens to these old horses when they get like this?" I told him they usually get weak enough that they lay down and then are unable to get back up. I also told him we usually end up putting them to sleep. We drove away and did whatever we were going to do.

Early the next morning, before I left to go over to their ranch, David called me from his mobile phone and told me the old horse was down and that I needed to bring whatever I needed to put him to sleep, because he looked bad. I told him I would come prepared to treat or euthanize the horse. The old horse had lain down with his feet and legs pointed slightly uphill and was unable to get up because of the position of his feet. He had been in that position and attempting to rise for a couple of hours before they came to work and found him. David and Frank both told me to do whatever I thought I could, but to put him to sleep if that would be best.

I examined the horse and gave him a pain killer. With some help, I was then able to get him laying up on his chest with his legs under him instead of flat out on his side. The horse was so weak, he couldn't pick his muzzle up off the ground. I gave him a few minutes to see if there would be any indication that he still had some energy or will to fight, but he appeared to get even weaker. I determined in my own mind that he would never get up again, so I went back to the truck and got the medication to put him down.

As I approached the old horse, I looked at his overall condition again. There he was in a normal laying position; thin, rough hair coat, abrasions on his head, hips, and muzzle from trying to get up. His muzzle was resting on the ground. I approached him from his left side (the side with the blind eye), slipped the needle into his vein, and gave the injection to put him to sleep. He never moved, but his breathing stopped, and I listened to his chest as his heart slowed to a stop. He was still in the same position, and from a short distance, you could tell no difference from two minutes before, when he was still alive. Before I turned to walk away, I kneeled and listened one last time and determined that his heart had indeed stopped, and then I looked back toward his head as I stood back up.

From the blind eye that had been that way for years, came three tear drops, one after another, and they fell to the ground in the same spot.

Putting an animal to sleep is sad any time, but that animal struck me as being particularly sad. Maybe it was because it belonged to friends of mine, or maybe it was because the tears fell from an eye that had not seen anything for years. I really don't know why it had that effect on me.

I thought about the horse periodically over the next few days, and several thoughts came to my mind.

The horse was not pretty, had lost a lot of weight, and was wounded on his hips, head, and muzzle from trying to get up. He had an eye which had been blind for years, and his heart had stopped—he was dead.

We have all seen people who are not pretty and who are wounded due to the sinful way they have lived their lives. We know that they are blind to the truth and have been that way for years. We know their physical heart is still beating, but they are so stubborn we believe their spiritual heart must have stopped years ago. We have long ago given up on trying to show them the goods news of Christ. We know they are hopeless. But are they?

I guess the old horse taught me something that day. He was dead, but I learned something. When we look at people and believe from their past actions and their present condition that they are spiritually blind and dead, we need to take that one last look. As long as that person can still shed tears that fall to the ground, then the message of Christ still has a chance to be effective in their lives, and we are responsible for extending a hand and telling the story of Christ.

Would We Be Recognized?

The other day, I was going to be working outside, so I dressed in my old boots, jeans that were faded and slightly stained, and a well-worn blue work shirt. I drove to a store that sells farm and ranch supplies to get a couple of hog panels to finish a pig pen.

I went into the store, got a small feed pan, and then went to the checkout counter and told the lady I also needed two hog panels. She rang up the total, and as I was paying her, another employee came to the counter. The other employee has known me a number of years, and he began to ask me questions about veterinary medicine. We had a short discussion about a particular medication. Up until that point, the lady who checked me out had no idea I was a veterinarian.

If that lady had come into my place of business, she would have known in a very short time that I am a veterinarian. She would have known it by my being in a veterinary clinic and my actions and speech. In the farm supply store, dressed as I was, she had no way of knowing my profession. I wondered if a person who did not know me would know I was a Christian. Would they see it by my actions and deeds, or would they only be able to see it when I was gathered with this group on Sunday?

How can we show faith in our lives without being so overbearing that we push people further from the savior they so desperately need to know? Can we live in a manner that will allow us to be known for what we are, even when we are out of our usual setting? Hopefully we can.

How To Live

Enjoy the good times when the sun is shining on you.
Endure the bad times when there are dark clouds all around.
Tell the truth simply and plainly, and let criticism fall where it may.
Do good, and be good.
Keep close to God.

Be Thankful

Did you thank the man who plowed the ground?
That from which he was made.
He plowed it deep to catch the rain in a deep layer of
clay.
He did it under the sun, in the field, while others rested
in the shade.

Did you thank the faithful woman? His wife beside him.
From his body, by God, she was taken, so in times of
trial he would not be shaken.
She stood beside him, so together they were strong, to
endure
the days when they were long.

Together they toil, and make a living from the soil,
just as God said man must do.
Over the years they endure the strain, while providing
for many,
though families like theirs are few.

How do they endure, when with each passing year they
look
around to see that families like theirs are fewer?
Listen and you will know when you hear prayers to God
around a supper table, next to a bed on bended knee,
or in a pickup on a dusty turn row.

Be thankful then, for the women, children, and men
who
work in the fields so you will have food to eat and
clothes
to wear.
For someday you may turn around to find, that no one is
working there.

Tradition and Ambition

Any time we put our tradition or personal ambition and desire above love and respect for other people, we are wrong.

Cat Fights

Cats have well marked territories where they roam. There is harmony between neighbors when, out of fear or respect, borders between territories are not violated.

There was an old, well-respected cat who had an area that had been clearly marked for years. He and his neighbors respected one another, and he believed he would hand this territory over to the right successor when the time came.

One of his neighbors was a young, well-respected cat who admired the old cat. After a number of years, the young cat began to wonder why the old cat didn't step aside and let him take his place. In his mind, the old cat had a lot of power and a larger territory. In reality, they were about the same size.

One day the young cat decided to test the old cat by violating the edge of his territory. The old cat noticed and wondered why the young cat didn't show him more respect. The young cat wondered why the old cat did not show him more respect and allow changes that would be suitable to him. One day there was a confrontation, and it was clear that neither cat would come out unharmed.

When cats fight there is a lot of growling. At first, it is done from a distance. Then, as they creep closer, the growling becomes higher pitched and louder. Finally, when they are face to face and staring at each other, the growling has become a shriek. At this point there is no retreat, because if one cat turns to run, he is attacked from the rear.

The young cat made another "testing" invasion into the old cat's territory. They faced off and stared at one another to see who would blink and run, or who would strike the first blow in a nasty fight. The two cats could feel one another's breath as they shrieked. You really couldn't tell who struck the first blow, but there was a long, hard fight, and the young cat won due to physical stamina. He struck the old cat one last time, across the top of his hips, as he turned to run away. The young cat could feel the sting of the wounds on his face. This was the first time he had tangled with such a skilled and worthy foe (if that is really what he was).

The young cat never saw the old cat again. He didn't know where the old cat went, he just didn't see him any more. He claimed the old cat's territory and even held on to his own territory. He managed the large territory well for a number of years, because he was a hard worker and saw to it that things were done his way by the surrounding neighbors. He felt good about himself and his accomplishments.

Periodically there were small misunderstandings and spats, during which he would feel the sting of wounds on his face. He always won, and never felt the sting of a wound across the top of his hips from turning and running from a fight. He was beginning to slow down a little, but the other cats respected him enough to not bother him. He thought he would stay on a while longer and then peacefully turn his territory over to some young, deserving cat.

One day he saw a young cat from an adjacent territory in his area. He thought it was something that could be handled with reasoning or a small spat. When stares and growling did not resolve the problem, they crept closer and closer together, until they were face to face and could feel one another's breath as they shrieked. A long, hard fight started, and the new cat won due to more stamina. For the first time, he felt the sting of a wound across the top of his hips that the young cat inflicted as he ran away. He wandered off and died.

The cat had died, but he suddenly realized he was in a different world. It was a spiritual world, and he was face to face with the one who would be his judge. He turned around to see he was surrounded by a lot of other cats whose faces were scarred, bleeding, and swollen. To his dismay and shame, he realized they all had an open, bleeding wound across their hips ... just like his. He even saw the cat from whom he had won his earthly territory.

Finally, the judge spoke: "Look around at yourselves. How can you claim to be my children? I came to your realm, showed you how to live, and you even had a record of my life and how I taught you to live. The only real power you have on earth comes from your heart. That power can only be used for good as I allow it to flow through you. I only asked you to love God, love one another, and love your neighbor as yourself."

The cat took one last look around at all the painful, bleeding wounds and hung his head in shame.

Choices

If I have chosen to live a Christian life and do good in my walk on this earth, someone will know where I have been.

Whether I have chosen to live as a Christian and do good or have chosen to do evil on this earth, God will surely know where I have been.

Randy

Randy walked through the door of the one place in town he would find someone he knew. He had on a dirty cap, old shirt, and an old pair of pants. On his feet were a pair of slippers. He had been at the beach, sleeping in his pickup, for two days, without bathing or changing clothes. The stench of cigarette smoke was in his clothes.

Randy was less than fifty, and yet the lines in his face and the texture of his skin spoke of a hard life. His smile revealed the missing and broken teeth behind chapped lips that were surrounded with three or four days' growth of his beard. His hair curled from under the edge of his cap, and his paralyzed right arm hung from a dirty sling around his neck. His unusual walk was due to partial paralysis of his right leg.

A number of years ago, a stroke and a heart attack had changed his life. Randy's body was less functional, and his memory and speech had been altered, which made communication difficult. Ruthless people would often take advantage of him, because he was just as likely to hand someone a fifty or twenty for a three dollar purchase as he was to give them a five.

Several years ago, an old friend, Ray, had taken him into his home for several months, tried to help him where he could, and spent some time talking with him about Jesus. Randy finally became restless and moved on. Ray had moved, and several months later, Randy came back to town and found a friend he'd met while living with Ray. Randy picked up some personal belongings and left again. Now, after nearly a year, he showed up and found the friend at work.

Randy stayed around for a couple of hours, and finally the friend made some telephone calls and took a lunch break with Randy. They stopped at a garage and left Randy's old Chevy pickup for a tune-up. The friend took him to a barber shop, where he left him for a shampoo (to get the sand out of his hair), a hair cut, and a mustache trim. The friend came back a few minutes later to find someone who looked a great deal different. As usual, Randy handed the barber numerous bills, folded over, to count out the right amount.

They contacted Ray, who picked Randy up after work, and they went to get his pickup. A couple of hours later, Randy was back on the road toward home. Ray and his friend wondered when he would be back again.

Who is this man whose body and mind have been ravaged by hard living, a heart attack, and a stroke? He is your brother…your brother in Christ. You see, the first time he came to see Ray, he came to understand about God and Love and Jesus. He was baptized, and many of you smiled and clapped when it was announced at church. It didn't change him on the outside, but inwardly he was changed. The big change was in his heart, where he came to understand the love of God. He came to that understanding because Ray took care of his physical and spiritual needs.

To most of us, Randy may have looked more like a beach bum than a brother in Christ. But, there was also a time when a beaten and exhausted man, near death, and hanging on a cross didn't look much like a king.

Families (Mom and Dad)

Following are some thoughts about families. Specifically, about parents, children, and the ramifications of trouble between parents and the trouble it causes for children. I am not an expert on such matters, but I have seen the results in the lives of many people, and it breaks my heart. I have seen the torn lives in the families of close relatives, have prayed for those people regularly, and feel so helpless in trying to preserve something that desperately needs to be saved. I also pray for myself that such things will not happen to my personal family, because it seems we are all vulnerable.

What does a child need to develop into a healthy adult? Children need the influence of both parents…living together under the same roof. A father has a special way of nurturing a child that a mother does not have, and a mother has a special way of nurturing a child that a father does not have. A child may need both of those kinds of nurturing at the same time. I'll give an example: A child wakes up crying in the middle of the night because they thought they heard an unusual noise. The mother wakes up and goes to the child first, then calls the father. The mother calms and soothes the child so he or she can talk, and when he finds out about the noise, the father is able to instill confidence in the child because the father checks to see where the noise might have come from. The mother calms and soothes the child while the father checks out the noise. When the father comes back into the room, he is able to lay the child's fears to rest, and the mother is able to softly get the child back to sleep. The noise may or may not have existed.

There was no substitute for the father. He was able, by his very nature, to instill confidence into the child in a way the mother could not, even though he may have been nearly as scared as the child. There was something about the way he was able to nurture the child in that moment that instilled confidence into the child.

There was no substitute for the mother. She was able, by her very nature, to provide that soft, tender, loving touch that soothed the child and allowed the child to go back to sleep.

That child needed the influence of both parents at that very moment. Talking about it with mom or dad on the telephone or the next day falls far short of the nurturing needed by that child. Yet, all across America, children are forced to wait for the nurturing they need from an absent parent. Very often they only get an answering machine when they are forced to call. That is tragic and hurts me down in my innermost being. Parents turn and walk away, searching for happiness that is supposed to be "out there" somewhere. Even Christ said, "in this world you will have trouble."

Something else is also happening all across America. Fathers and mothers are staying under the same roof, together, even though what they have may not be something most people would call happiness. They are involved in the great struggle to make things work, because they want their children to have a life at least as good as theirs, and hopefully, better than theirs. There are fathers going home to their families, even when they don't feel like it, and there are mothers going home to their families, even when they don't feel like it. They do it because they know it is the right thing to do, even when others around them are acting happy when they are doing what is wrong and not going home to their families.

We are all sacrificing our lives, one day at a time, for something. Can you think of anything more worthwhile on this earth for which to sacrifice your life than your children? I can't. Our children are our link to the future, our legacy. How do we measure a successful life? By houses, cars, or money? We will only have a legacy of success if people look at our lives and love and respect our God and love and respect our children.

I only hope that I can live my life for the right goals so someday I might hear the words, "well done, good and faithful servant."

Family Reunion
(After Fred Had Gone)

We took a trip just the other day.
Not on a boat or train,
But on the wings of a fast jet plane.

We traveled half way across the country
To see our roots,
And didn't even wear any cowboy boots.

The trip was fine,
And didn't take much time.
And folks were waiting at
The end of the line.

We set out from Columbia,
And rode a while,
Arrived in Hartsville,
A little tired, but with a smile.

We gathered with family,
Had a bite to eat,
But it really felt good, that evening,
When the pillow touched our cheek.

The next morning we loaded in the van,
Taking a trip southeast, to Darlington,
To see something grand.

We arrived at Oaklyn Plantation,
Without hesitation,
Got out of the van and
Began our visitation.

We saw a house where the
Allen family used to stay,
Then toured the grand
Plantation house across the way.

You could feel the history
In the soil beneath your feet,
And sense it in the air you breathed, and
In the warm sun against your cheeks.

We had trod a part of the path
Of the generation before.
For a moment the sounds rang clearer,
Of the family stories and folklore.

How they survived we really don't know.
Except on love that in their hearts glowed.
"They did it by hard work," one might say,
Fact be known it was love from the heavenly way.

Now one is gone,
And five remain.
He is living where there is no pain.
He has passed through, and there will stay.
Waiting for us in the land of endless day.

Though we cry in pain when the days are dark.
We feel the presence of his loving heart.
And see his smile and blue eyes,
As he looks on us from the other side.
He and Mama, and Daddy, and Viv
Are visiting about the lives they lived.
And how, from the land they made a
Living on this earth.

And Jimmie, and Gary,
And all those gone before
Were there to greet him,
As he walked through the door.

It was a grand reunion,
And will be better yet,
When all those still here,
Go on, and with the Savior have met.

Christ will greet the others when they come,
With a "good and faithful servant, 'Welcome'"
As one by one they go to stay,
In the land with no night, but never-ending day.

And there may be a surprise for the five
Who once were six.
When they find in that land,
Everyone plays cars with a whole brick.

No whole ones, halves, and "have nots."
Like on earth seemed to be their lot.
They understand it really doesn't matter
Where they stood, here, on the economic ladder.

They knew about the important things,
About love, laughter, and learning how to sing.
About singing praises to
Jesus, their lord and king.
They learned it from people in the
Room next to theirs.
At bedtime, when they saw their parents
Get down on knees to say their prayers.

They learned about commitment to husband and wife,
As they struggled to make ends meet in this hard life.
They saw how those two humbled themselves before God,
Even as on this earth a rugged path they trod.

Listen closely, and you can hear cheers,
As each one goes at the end of his years.
They're clapping, and yelling, and rooting for us,
As our earthly, mortal bodies go back to dust.

The dust from which we were made,
And on this earth we turned with a spade.
To feed the thirsting and hunger
Which never ceased, but only for a while would fade.

So as we live our lives, while here,
Listen closely for that heavenly cheer.
And remember in whom the two on their
Knees placed their trust.

For it is the most important thing
They passed on to us.
That in God and Jesus our savior,
We need to trust.

To know how to live our daily lives,
Even when tears flow down our cheeks from our eyes.
Knowing He will wipe them all away,
When we leave this earth, and go with Him,
For eternity to stay.

What Are You Going to Be?

During our lives, people often ask, "What are you going to be?" "What are you going to study?" or "What are you going to do?" After having worked in the same profession for twenty-seven years, those are not questions people ask me. I guess the real question at this point is, "What is best for me to be?"

It would probably be best if I were a moon. Being a moon, maybe people would see my reflection and be drawn closer until they would turn and see the source. Then they would see the beauty, the power, and the glory of The Son. Hopefully, people see the light I reflect in living daily for God.

Church/Tractor

Organized religion and a tractor are a great deal alike. They both give us the power to do things we could not do on our own. Organized religion gives us the ability to cultivate love, harmony, and spiritual development in the lives of many people at the same time. A tractor allows an individual to cultivate a lot of plants at one time. With one, we are able to produce abundant spiritual growth and spiritual fruit, due to the power of the church, and with the other, we are able to cultivate plants to produce abundant crops in the field. Used properly, both can lead to a bountiful spiritual growth to nurture the soul and a bountiful food crop to nurture the body. But, we must be careful how we use them.

With a tractor cultivating crops, you have to maintain your focus and attention constantly, and you have to keep your eye on the purpose and goal and stop periodically to see how you are doing. You often have to make adjustments in speed, depth, and position of the sweeps in order to help nurture the crop. Without constant attention and adjustments, you may do more harm than good to the crop you are cultivating.

With the church cultivating spiritual development in the lives of people, it is equally important to maintain our focus and attention on the ultimate goal. It is also important to stop and see how we are doing, periodically, to see if there needs to be some adjustment in speed and direction in order to properly cultivate the spirit and allow people to develop to their full potential.

In the church, and in the field, it is important to be careful how we use the power given to us. We must remain focused and at the same time be aware of what is going on around us in order to make adjustments along the way. It would be tragic to get to the other end and discover that our misuse of powerful tools has cut off, at the roots, the very lives and crops we were trying to cultivate. Not only did we not nurture and help, we destroyed those lives so they were never able to produce fruit of the spirit or bountiful food for the body.

Christianity

Christianity is a whole lot bigger than the Church of Christ, the Methodist, Catholic, Presbyterian, Baptist, Episcopal, and Lutheran churches combined.

Go to Botswana, Zambia, Chile, Argentina, Bolivia, Australia, New Zealand, New Guinea, Korea, and Thailand, and go to a gathering of Christians. Take away all of the external things we use to identify ourselves: signs, statues, robes, hats, stained glass windows, dancing, or lack of it. Put aside instrumental music, waving, and clapping of hands, and just listen to the spoken message. After hearing the message of Jesus Christ, do you think you would be able to tell which organized church group originally evangelized the group of Christians with whom you were meeting? You might or might not be able to tell.

The body of Christ is very, very large, and we have no more power to keep it confined by our external restrictions than Satan had power to keep Christ confined to the cross or in the grave. We must be aware of the size of the body of Christ and realize we may have more brothers and sisters in Christ than we can imagine.

Focus

We, as a people, need to stop looking into the mirror and at our immediate, material surroundings.

We need to look into the heart of Jesus and open our eyes to see the beauty and power of the love of God in His creation all around us.

July 4, 2000

Today, I took a day away from what I do on most Tuesdays. I got up and went to work on the farm of a friend.

They were harvesting grain, and I went to the field to drive a tractor, disking down stalks after the combines had been over the field. I checked the tractor, and one of the other workers came by to fill the tractor with fuel. I drove to the far end of the field and went to work.

From where I was working, I could see the other workers getting the combines ready to start harvesting after the dew had dried from the grain. A yellow, agricultural airplane was spraying a cotton field across the road.

Here I was, working with a good tractor on a good farm for good people. I thought about how fortunate I was to be able to do such a thing. You see, I go to the field when I can, to get back in touch with the reality of what it takes for us to have food and fiber which support us in our daily lives. Very few people actually work in agricultural production in our nation today, and it is by going to the field, periodically, that I am reminded of how hard some people work to supply the needs of most of the rest of the population. It makes me appreciate what I have and appreciate what farm workers do on a daily basis. I'm sure they do not fully understand the role they play in the lives of so many other people.

When I am in the field, on a tractor, I also am reminded of the bountiful harvests of the past, and crop failures due to drought. It makes me wonder how farmers can do what they do year after year. I am aware of, but really know very little about the harsh reality of expensive equipment, low prices, and the hard work and worry associated with farming. How farmers endure such things, I do not know…unless they have more faith than the rest of us.

Farmers have tremendous trust in the people with whom they work, and they must have tremendous faith in God to take care of them in the areas of their lives over which they have no control. They toil and earn their living from the earth…the same earth from which we were made, and to which we will return at the end of our lives in this world. I believe there is a special place for people who earn their living and serve others by working the land. I will go the field as often as I can to gain some small appreciation for those who work the land on a daily basis.

Thanks to all of you.

Making It through the Storm

She was born in the summer of her twenty-first year.
And began to smile…almost from ear to ear.
Down her cheeks, at times, flowed a stream of tears.
When she realized she had almost walked into her greatest fear.
That of being bound to an untrue heart.

Seven long years ago she was told to leave.
Under conditions, and by people, most of us
Could never understand or believe.
She was told to look for someone to love,
But was never told to look above.

The Savior wept many bitter tears.
When he saw how His child had been treated,
And held His loving arms around her
To protect, guard, and calm all her fears.
He even provided a special person to live next door.
Kind of a mother hen to spread her wings to protect
His precious child when all around, the storms of life did roar.

When there were dangers all around,
And most other people would have been knocked to the ground.
She managed to stand strong,
Even when the days and nights were long.
And when others told her to give in,
She hung on, gritted her teeth, and stuck out her chin.
Tenacity and determination she possessed,
Even in a life filled with danger and distress.

With some time now, the clouds will begin to clear.
As she comes out of darkness and into the light,
And can see the Savior in His great might.
Once she understands Him and knows He is near.
She can look to the future without fear.

And one day when the time is right,
He will provide for her someone who lives in the light.
Someone who will treat her with gentle love and respect,
And the love of God, his heart will reflect.
They will be bound, in the sight of God,
To live on this earth where His precious Son once trod.
And when their lives on this earth are ended,
They will go to their heavenly home so splendid,
To live with Him, who on this earth, her fears finally ended.

Devil's Claw

A few weeks ago I drove a tractor, shredding cotton stalks. When I was going to a new field, the farmer told me to stop the tractor when I saw a Devil's Claw, pull or chop it with a hoe, and carry it to the end to be stacked so they could haul them out of the field.

Devil's Claw is a weed with relatively large, pale green leaves, and a bloom that can add beauty to the plant. It has a large, single stalk that divides into two main branches a short distance above the ground. The stem is hollow, and bad smelling sap gets on your hands when you touch the plant. The seed pod is streamlined and has a neat appearance when green, but splits into two long talons when it dries and matures.

The farmer wanted me to pull the weeds to keep from scattering the plants by shredding. The plants are not in every field on the farm and were originally brought in on equipment by cotton harvesters from another part of the state.

It took an hour to chop the weeds and haul them to the end of the field to be stacked. During that hour, time was lost on the main task at hand, and I had to get off and back on the tractor numerous times. I also ended up with a puncture or two in my fingers from the seed pods and had the sticky smelly sap on my hands and clothes.

Once I was on the tractor in a clean part of the field, I was able to think about the weed and the name, "Devil's Claw."

Among the plants of the field, it really wasn't ugly and didn't look like anything to fear or avoid. The pale green color, bloom, size of the plant, and its leaves are not unattractive. The green seed pod is sort of neat due to its shape. It is very much like some of the things that are attractive to us in life, which makes the name of the plant appropriate.

Like a lot of things which are not good for us, we do not see anything on the surface that makes us think we should avoid it. Once we are around it, either due to our own actions or the actions of someone else, we can never be completely free from its effects.

As with other evil things, it takes valuable time from our goals in life. It is attractive enough, but when handled, we are contaminated with the bad odor. It is also hollow, just like promises of evil things in this world. When the seed pod matures, it has long talons that hook onto you, causing injury. It spreads to other parts of your life, sprouting at the next opportunity.

If I don't have Devil's Claw in the field of my life, I should stay away and be on guard against it. If I recognize Devil's Claw in the field of my life, I should cut and haul it to the end to be stacked and burned.

Christian Service

Do you ever become impatient when listening to someone? Do you think their thoughts and words are things you do not need to know?

You are right. You probably don't need to hear what they have to say. But think about one thing: The other person may have a tremendous need for someone to listen.

Be patient, particularly if the person speaking is very young or very old. In that moment, there may be no higher form of Christian service than listening to the heart and soul of another child of God.

The Best Way to Live

The best way to live your life on this side of death is to know The One who will determine how you live on the other side of death.

August 17, 2003

I stayed up late last night visiting with family and friends, so I slept a little later than usual this morning. I had planned to go to Sunday school and church. Shortly after I got up, the telephone rang. It was a worker at a dairy farm twenty-five miles from here.

Maggie told me they had a cow unable to calve. The calf had already died, and they were unable to deliver it. Anytime I receive a call from Maggie and they cannot deliver a calf, I know it will be a difficult delivery because the workers on this dairy are good at delivering a calf. I was tired and not looking forward to what I was going to do, but I put on my old clothes, ate a small bowl of cereal, and headed out to the farm. There was very little traffic so the drive through the countryside was quiet, and I drove through patchy fog on the way. As I arrived at the dairy, Maggie directed me to the pens.

I got my equipment in a bucket, splashed some antiseptic on it, got down on my knees behind the cow, and went to work. The calf was just a little too large for its front legs and head to pass through the pelvis of the cow at the same time. Since the calf had already died, I did a partial fetotomy and was able to deliver the calf without having to do a C-section on the cow. Maggie and Alex helped by handing tools and lubricant to me, and we visited as I worked on the cow. After removing the calf, I placed some medicated boluses into the cow's uterus, and gave Maggie and Alex instructions about medications to use over the next few days.

During conversation, Maggie asked me if I had been getting ready to go to church. I told her "Yes," and when I finished cleaning my equipment, she asked me what time church started. I told her I would miss Sunday school but could still make it to church services. She told me she didn't go to church often, due to work, but she stopped by the church building and left a contribution on the steps. Before I left, she said she hoped I made it to church on time. Several other workers were milking cows, feeding calves, and tending to the cow we treated. On the way home, I saw a cotton picker and cotton module builder going down the road to work in a cotton field later in the day.

I made it to church services on time. I had showered and put on clean clothes, and the people at church didn't know where I had been or what sort of work I had done that morning.

Thoughts of Maggie, Alex, other workers at the dairy, and people involved with the cotton harvest stayed with me for the next few days. Here were people who work close to the earth, see new life and death periodically, and work at times when the rest of us are usually off. I saw an older woman in the milk room that morning who has worked her whole life cleaning and filling bottles with milk and feeding calves. These people do work necessary for the rest of us to have food to eat and fiber to make the clothes we wear.

Maggie seldom gets to go to church, but she was doing what she could by leaving a contribution at the church building on her way to work. And yet, what was her concern that morning? Her concern was that I make it to church on time. Very basically, her concern was for my spiritual well being. People of the earth are such a blessing to me under those circumstances. I was there to help them by helping the cow. It involved me being on my knees behind the cow, in cedar bedding and dirt, covered in birth fluids, blood, and obstetrical lubricant. I even said a silent prayer the procedure would be successful.

Later, I was able to make it to church services and hear a good lesson. I missed Sunday school class that morning, but I had already worshiped, with the people of the earth, by taking care of animals and serving others before going to the church building. I am truly thankful to God for that part of the congregation.

Follow Your Heart

Each one is born in a space and time
With their heart and soul connected to mine.
It is all a part of His design…
The One not bound by space and time.

He sent a part of Himself to earth
And entered this world through a lowly birth.
They came to see Him in the manger where He lay.
The One who came to show us the way.

Through our hearts we are joined to Him above,
And surrounded with His majestic love.
To each one of us is given
A heart on this earth to whom we are driven.

It is through His love, and not by fate
That we each find our earthly mate.
With simple promises we join our lives,
Beneath the gaze of His loving and watchful eyes.

And finally, when we have done our part,
Through death we are taken back to His heart.
To a place not bound by space and time,
Where He speaks to His own in a voice so kind.

For the heart bound to the one taken,
Unseen truth soothes separation.
Knowing he, too, will be called back
To the place not bound by time and space.

So even in sorrow we can seek His favor,
And be thankful for Jesus, our Savior.
For we know He is always there,
To hear the most simple, whispered prayer.

In this season of colored lights burning,
Let us follow our heart's true yearning.
To seek out that which in our heart is burning.
And allow our souls to be found,
In the heart of the living God.

Planting Seed/Going Home
(December 22, 2002)

Today, I went to Papalote to repair fence on the creek down by the bridge. The repairs took a couple of hours, and shortly before I finished, Warren's family walked by. They asked if I needed Warren to come help with the fence, but I was nearly finished. As I drove back by the Miller's place, I noticed there was nothing growing in the garden. I saw Warren outside and pulled into their driveway on the tractor. I asked if they could use a few turnips out of our garden, and he said he would be down in a few minutes to get them.

My parents and Warren's parents have known one another for more than forty years. My parents bought a piece of property down the road from the Millers a number of years ago, and they have been good neighbors. They have traded produce and pecans from the garden and helped one another periodically when needed. In short, they put their faith into practice, helping each other through the years. Now they are all older than seventy-five, and Warren and I do most of the work on their respective places.

After offering the turnips to Warren, I drove back to my parents' place; down the lane, past the garden, and to the barn. A few minutes later, I looked up to see Mr. Miller coming down the driveway, on his riding mower with a small two wheeled cart in tow. I went to the garden and said, "Hi," opened the garden gate, and began to pull turnips big enough to eat. Mr. Miller followed me and put the turnips in a bucket as I pulled them and shook dirt from the roots. Mr. Miller asked me how my dad was doing, and I said, "He's not doing any good.," and he replied, "That's so sad." My dad has developed mental illness over the last year, and has good and bad days, but is getting progressively worse.

As Mr. Miller put his bucket on the cart, my mother walked out to the garden, and they began to visit. I left them in conversation and used the tractor to put some limbs on a brush pile. As I drove back to the barn and stopped, I stayed on the tractor for a minute longer and observed. To my right was a grove of pine trees my dad planted thirty years ago. On the right side of the driveway, in the barn yard, was the small fenced-in garden, and straight ahead was an old windmill tower. In a curve of the driveway stood my mother and Mr. Miller still visiting. In a pasture beyond the windmill were three heifers, and in the pasture next to the lane that leads out to the road stood a group of cows with young and newborn calves. It was a cool, overcast day, and I felt an occasional drop of rain on my skin. My focus returned to my mother and Mr. Miller.

His riding mower was facing the garden, and the cart extended toward my left. Mr. Miller was standing behind the cart with his back to it, and my mother was facing him. Mr. Miller is a big, tall man, and he leaned forward on a walking cane with his left hand gripping the edge of his vest which was open in the front. He had on a cap, a dark brown, long sleeved shirt. His vest was medium blue, and his pants were dark blue. Mama is short and had on black pants, a long sleeved white shirt, and a red vest. I enjoyed seeing the two of them, as he leaned forward on his cane, and she gestured with her hands as they talked. I will forever have the picture of that moment in my memory.

As I drove the tractor in their direction, they ended the conversation and Mr. Miller turned and walked back to his mower, painfully stiff as he moved. Mama turned and walked toward the house, and I slowed the tractor to let her get through the gate before I drove up the lane to mow the ditch along the road. At the gate I turned left and began to mow. At the end of the property, I turned back toward the gate. As I came around a curve in the road, I saw Mr. Miller, on his mower, headed back down the side of the road. He was a solitary figure ahead of me, headed toward home with fresh turnips in a bucket on the cart he towed.

I thought about Mr. and Mrs. Miller and my parents. They have been, and are still good neighbors. They are not people who are always visiting in one another's home, but they have shared a glass of iced tea together on occasion and have a key to one another's gate. They would help one another at any time. Their Christian walks have not been down the exact same path, but they do have faith and have truly loved God and loved their neighbors as themselves. They are now closer to being with God than ever before. Warren and I are willing to cooperate and help one another partly because of the tremendous example set before us. We are reaping a harvest from seed they have sown.

I seldom eat turnips, but I do like to grow and share them with others. Without them, this would have been just another cool, overcast December day. Because of those few turnips, I was able to see two people, from the generation before, pictured in a setting I will never forget. Mr. and Mrs. Miller and Mama and Papa have set a good example, as we watch them ahead of us, going down the road toward home....

Printed in the United States
38249LVS00002B/19-117